MW00940208

The Lawyer Who Leapt

It's Wednesday morning, September 24th to be precise, and Tom Jarrell is in love.

He's walking through the tree-covered streets of Daytona Beach, on his way to work, and thinking about the wonderful night he just spent.

But, when he gets to the office, he realizes he has a few things that need to be done.

For one, he needs to file an affidavit in a murder trial, but he's never done any such thing, so he heads off to his old law school to meet with his favorite professor from before the war to get some much-needed advice. And, while there, he gets much more than he was expecting.

Meanwhile, Ronnie Grisham is in trouble with his landlady. He hasn't slept in his boarding house bed for two nights and she just read her cards last night. Change is coming. Could the cards be pointing to Ronnie?

As for Marveen Dodge, her suspicions about what is really going on at the law office of Tom Jarrell, Esquire, is like a simmering pot that could boil over at any moment.

And, Alice Watson is doing just fine, thank you very much, and looking forward to a nice Saturday at the beach with her girl.

But, none of them expects what happens next as two mysterious girls arrive in town, suitcases in hand... And an unexpected trial gets underway...

Read about all of this, and more, in the case of *THE LAWYER WHO LEAPT*.

The Lawyer Who Leapt

Nick Williams Mysteries

The Unexpected Heiress

The Amorous Attorney

The Sartorial Senator

The Laconic Lumberjack

The Perplexed Pumpkin

The Savage Son

The Mangled Mobster

The Iniquitous Investigator

The Voluptuous Vixen

The Timid Traitor

The Sodden Sailor

The Excluded Exile

The Paradoxical Parent

The Pitiful Player

The Childish Churl

The Rotten Rancher

A Happy Holiday

The Adroit Alien

The Leaping Lord

The Constant Caprese

The Shameless Sodomite

The Harried Husband

The Stymied Star

The Roving Refugee

The Perfidious Parolee

The Derelict Dad

Nick & Carter Stories

An Enchanted Beginning

Golden Gate Love Stories

The One He Waited For

Their Own Hidden Island

Daytona Beach Stories

The Sailor Who Washed Ashore

The Lawyer Who Leapt

The Lawyer Who Leapt

Daytona Beach

Book 2

By Frank W. Butterfield

Published With Delight

By The Author

MMXVIII

The Lawyer Who Leapt

ISBN-10: 1731385242
ISBN-13: 978-1731385246

First publication: November 2018

This book contains explicit language
and suggestive situations.

This is a work of fiction that refers to historical figures, locales, and events, along with many completely fictional ones. The primary characters are utterly fictional and do not resemble anyone that I have ever met or known of.

Be the first to know about new releases:

frankwbutterfield.com

DB02-B-20181115

Contents

[T]he story here will be told by more than one pen, as the story of an offense against the laws is told in Court by more than one witness—with the same object, in both cases, to present the truth always in its most direct and most intelligible aspect; and to trace the course of one complete series of events, by making the persons who have been most closely connected with them, at each successive stage, relate their own experience, word for word.

—Wilkie Collins

The Woman In White

Prologue

Affidavit of Mrs. Inez Johnson
Tuesday, September 23, 1947

My name is Mrs. Inez Johnson. My husband is Mr. Leland Johnson. He is the President of Fidelity Trust Bank at 270 North Beach Street, Daytona Beach, Florida. We live at 301 North Halifax Avenue, Daytona Beach, Florida.

On the evening of Saturday, September 6, 1947, my husband told me that our son, Roland (herein referred to as Skipper), had agreed to no longer see his long-time friend Howard Kirkpatrick (herein referred to as Howie). My husband and I had been concerned for some time about the nature of their friendship. On several occasions, and starting in December of 1946, my husband had told Skipper that he believed that the two boys should not remain as close as they had been to that point. Skipper would usually agree but then take no action, much to his father's annoyance.

At some time before the sixth, my son arranged to have a friend, whose name I do not know, help him devise a plan where it would appear as though Skipper had disappeared from his fishing boat, the Mary Belle, in the Atlantic. He planned to convince Howie to go with him out into the open sea, on Sunday, the seventh, where he would attack Howie, knocking him unconscious and would then escape from the Mary Belle on this friend's speedboat.

Late on Sunday, the seventh, Skipper arrived at our home, having been driven there by this unknown friend. When I asked Skipper about the Mary Belle and Howie, he told me of his plan and its success. I asked him to report the boat as adrift to the Coast Guard and he refused. I then confronted my husband who insisted I remain quiet and let Howie make his own way back to land. My husband then told me he had arranged for Skipper to be married to the daughter of a business acquaintance, Mr. Roger G. Thompson, from Saint Augustine, Florida. Skipper and Pauline Thompson were to fly up to Atlanta from Saint Augustine in a private plane early on Monday, the fifteenth, and to be married there in Atlanta. My husband had arranged to buy a house in a fashionable part of that city for the two to live in as man and wife and for Skipper to begin a job at Southern Merchants Bank in downtown Atlanta. He also told me that Mr. Thompson had the same concern about Pauline and her friend, a girl whose name I do not know, as we had about Skipper and Howie.

I expressed my reservations about the legality of this plan, since I knew it might very well violate the Mann Act and was, in fact, tantamount to kidnapping since Pauline had not consented to leaving.

During the day of Monday, the eighth of September, I became increasingly worried when the Mary Belle was not seen coming through the inlet. My husband had hired a local of Ponce Park, whose name I do not know, to immediately telephone us when he saw it. On the early morning of Tuesday, the ninth, we received word that Howie had been seen piloting the Mary Belle through the inlet and was heading north up the Halifax River. Later that morning, I overheard my husband call Mr. Thomas Jarrell, an attorney retained by Howie, and question him about Skipper's whereabouts. When I looked into my husband's office, I observed Skipper watching his father carry on this conversation. To my eyes, Skipper was upset. I believe he may have been crying.

The next several days in our house were almost intolerable. My son moped around the house, obviously upset and, as the days passed, increasingly so. My husband refused to go into the office except for a couple of hours each morning and each afternoon, under the pretext that he was worried about Skipper, whom everyone believed to be lost at sea based on my husband's own slanderous lies.

I received call after call of condolences by well-meaning friends, both in person and over the telephone. Finally, I refused to answer any such inquiries, instructing my maid to turn all such callers away.

On the evening of Sunday, the fourteenth, my husband instructed my maid to pack a traveling bag for Skipper. He then forced our son to dress in an overcoat and, under cover of darkness, the two made their way to the marina where they boarded the Mary Belle.

I slept fitfully through the night. At approximately 5:30 in the morning, I was awakened by the sound of my husband returning. When I saw that he was carrying Skipper's traveling bag, I lost my mind for a brief while. Once I came to my senses, my husband told me they had fought and that Skipper had fallen into the ocean. Despite his best efforts, my husband claimed to have been unable to save Skipper before he drowned and his body sank. Later that morning, we received word from Daytona Beach Police Chief Thomas Johnson (no relation) that Skipper's body had been recovered north of Daytona Beach.

In spite of my husband's entreaties, I refused to attend the coroner's inquest or the opening day of Howie's trial.

I believed this version of my husband's story until this morning when I read of the testimony in open court that Skipper had been hit on the head with an oar. I rushed to DeLand, prepared to testify to the jury of all I knew, only to arrive in time to see the State's Attorney withdraw charges against Howie and to watch, in shame and horror, as my husband was led away by a bailiff for questioning.

I attest the previous to be true, to the best of my knowledge. I offer this affidavit of my own free will and do attest that none have coerced me to do so.

My forwarding address is care of my father, Dr. Lionel J. Markinson, 740 Park Avenue, New York, New York. I may also be reached by telephone in that city at TR3-2292.

Attested to this day, September 23, 1947, in Daytona Beach, Florida.

/s/ Mrs. Inez Johnson

So witnessed, September 23, 1947, in Daytona Beach, Florida.

/s/ Miss Marveen Dodge

/s/ Mr. Ronald H. Grisham

Chapter 1

761 S. Palmetto Avenue
Daytona Beach, Fla.
Wednesday, September 24, 1947
A quarter before 9 in the morning

Tom Jarrell whistled as he walked down Palmetto, headed to work. It was a beautiful morning, nice and cool following the previous day's tropical storm sideswipe. Tom felt as though fall might have arrived even though he knew better than to expect the kind of autumnal vision offered up in the Norman Rockwell covers of the *Saturday Evening Post*.

Tom didn't care, though. He was happy and deeply satisfied in a way he couldn't ever remember feeling before. As he strolled along, keeping out of the way of the occasional passing car, he thought about the night before, one where he and Ronnie Grisham had made a kind of passionate love that he never thought possible.

Back in April, his wife, Sarah, and their daughter, Missy, had been killed out on the DeLand Highway when a truck hit their car, head-on. After that, Tom had fallen apart. He'd begun to drink and stay drunk. After being fired from a local law firm, he'd finally realized he needed help.

So, he'd gotten on the train and headed to Chicago and then on into Wisconsin where he'd spent a few weeks at Lakeside Sanitarium under the care of Dr. Alexander Meisner. The good doctor had helped him come to terms with the tragedy he'd just been through and to find a way back from the edge of dipsomania. Since he'd returned to Daytona Beach, at the end of July, Tom hadn't had anything to drink. Or, not much.

One of the more intensive aspects of Dr. Meisner's therapy had been to tell Tom how his affection for Ronnie Grisham was a stunted expression of a desire for true male friendship. Instead of expressing that desire through sexual contact with Ronnie, Dr. Meisner had suggested Tom should maintain a cordial, but less intimate, friendship with the man.

Tom had tried that, but it had nearly driven him back to the bottle. Instead, and it would definitely have been frowned on by Dr. Meisner, Tom had taken up Ronnie's suggestion to start up a law practice. The two began to work together, opening up an office at 106A Beach Street, hiring Marveen Dodge to be their secretary, and taking on such clients as they could find.

That was how they'd met Howie Kirkpatrick, Tom's first important client. Howie had wandered in the office a few weeks earlier, afraid he'd murdered his best friend (and, as it turned out, his lover) out on the Atlantic. Tom and Ronnie were able to discover the truth and, just the day before, the charges against Howie had been dismissed.

Unfortunately, during his trial, word had gotten out about the nature of the relationship between Howie and Skipper Johnson. Tom had suggested the young man take a road trip up north and let the dust settle around town. Howie had agreed and, using Ronnie's car, had left town.

Over dinner the night before, Tom found himself unable to contain his passion for Ronnie any longer and they had spent the night rekindling an affair they'd had while Tom's wife, Sarah, was still alive and that truly began back in high school, in Tallahassee. According to Ronnie, she had known about their shared passions and had approved. That was news to Tom, but he tended to believe that Ronnie was telling him the truth.

Earlier that morning, Tom's maid, Alice, had walked into the house a little earlier than he was expecting. But, much to his surprise, she had been quite pleased that Tom and Ronnie had finally spent the night together. Tom was still not quite sure what to make of that, but the memory of her laughter on the other side of the bedroom door made him smile.

...

As Tom made his way to the top of the stairs just outside his office, he smiled one more time, thinking about Ronnie. The two had shared one lingering kiss in Tom's bedroom before Ronnie had left through the front door, taking Tom's car for the morning. All he would say, as he left, was that he had an important meeting. He didn't mention who it was with and Tom didn't care.

Opening the outer door of the office, Tom stopped short when he saw Marveen. She was sitting at her desk, her eyes glaring daggers at him as she did. Looking through the inner door that led into his office, Tom immediately understood why.

Sitting behind his desk, as if he owned the place, was Mr. Eugene Mayer, his former employer and mentor. Mr. Mayer was dressed in his usual seersucker suit, light blue, and had placed his straw hat in the middle of Tom's desk. The older man smiled at Tom and said, "Good morning."

Tom cautiously walked into his office. He removed his hat and his coat, hanging both on the rack, and stood about three feet from his desk. "Good morning, Mr. Mayer. How are you this morning?"

"Well, I'm fine, Tom." His smile broadened a bit. "Congratulations, my boy. You did a great job in court yesterday."

Tom nodded. "Thank you."

The older man waved his thanks away. "Don't mention it." He turned to his right and looked out the window above Beach Street. "Nice view you have of the river here. Better than mine, I can tell you that. Looks like they're making good progress on replacing the concrete bridge."

Still standing by his own desk, Tom said, "Yes, sir."

Looking up at him, Mr. Mayer asked, "Have you given any further thought to my proposal?"

Without hesitation, Tom replied, "I have and, as generous as it is, I'll have to take a pass."

Mr. Mayer's dark eyes narrowed. "Are you sure, son?"

Tom nodded. "Yes, sir. It's certainly very generous."

Looking around the office, Mr. Mayer said, "Well, I can't imagine how many years it will be before you make as much as I was offering you for just one year." He picked up his hat and then stood. "I'm afraid, Tom, that when I leave this office, I won't be able to offer you the job again. It's a take-it-or-leave-it kind of offer."

"Yes, sir. I understand."

Putting his hat on his head, the older man frowned. "I don't think you do."

Tom wasn't sure what to say in reply to that. When Mr. Mayer had offered to re-hire him two nights earlier, Tom knew it was as much a warning as anything else. He'd been summoned late on Monday night to the man's big house on the other side of the river. Mr. Mayer had offered him an annual salary of ten thousand dollars. Tom knew that the offer was an attempt on Mr. Mayer's part to keep him close. And, he could hear Ronnie from the night before, "you only do that with your enemies." Mr. Mayer saw him as a threat. Tom didn't know why, exactly, but he knew it was true.

As tempting as it was to go back to his old job, the truth was that he had plenty of money to stay afloat for a year or two without much business at all. The work had been coming in, in dribs and drabs. There was some interest about town in what he could offer as a lawyer.

Mr. Mayer puckered his mouth, like he did when he had a point to make, and said, "You see, Tom, in a town like Daytona Beach, there's only room for so many practicing attorneys. If you're in with Thornton and myself, there will always be plenty for you to do. In time, we'll bring you in as a partner and then, before you know it, you'll have a house on the river like mine." He smiled but there was nothing friendly in the expression. "Surely, you want to do well, don't you, son? I'm sure that's what Sarah would want."

Tom stiffened at the mention of his late wife's name. That was a low blow and further deepened his resolve to keep the law firm of Mayer & Thornton at a distance.

Forcing himself to smile, Tom said, "I appreciate your concern and your generosity, but I like working for myself."

Mr. Mayer walked around the desk and then stopped between Tom and the door. He turned and nodded. "I understand." He looked over towards the window facing the river. "One last chance, Tom." Keeping his eyes on the window, the older man sucked in through his teeth, something Tom remembered him doing when he was angry.

Tom shook his head. "No, sir, but thank you anyway."

Mr. Mayer nodded, turned, and walked through the door. He looked back at Marveen, who had been quietly sitting at her desk. Lifting his hat, he said, "Good morning, Miss Dodge." He walked through the open exterior door and quietly made his way down the steps. As soon as Tom heard the door at the foot of the stairs close, he breathed a sigh of relief.

Marveen stood and looked at Tom through the doorway. "What a creep."

Tom grinned a little, walked over to his desk, and sat in his chair. He looked at his secretary and asked, "How long was he here?"

She crossed her arms. "He was here when I got here. We need to change the locks."

Tom nodded thoughtfully. "Maybe. Or maybe Ronnie or I forgot to lock up when we left."

She shook her head. "Not likely. Ronnie always remembers to lock the door."

Tom sighed. "You're right." He leaned forward. "How was your date last night?"

Marveen blushed slightly. "We had a swell time. Bill is a great dancer. He took me to the Trocadero and we had dinner and danced." She sighed contentedly. "It was quite a night."

"I'm glad to hear it." Teasing her, he said, "That's two nights in a row."

She nodded. "Mother thinks I need to play a little hard to get, but I'm not getting any younger and I like Bill. He's nice." She looked up. "How'd you know Bill and I went out?"

"You look happy."

She smiled and nodded. "Oh! There was a telegram on the floor when I walked in this morning." She rolled her eyes. "I guess Mr. Mayer couldn't be bothered to pick it up."

"Who is it from?"

"Howie." She walked over to his desk and handed over a yellow envelope. "Did he leave town last night?"

Tom nodded. "Yes. I thought it best if he took a month or so and stayed away until all the gossip dies down." He pulled out the telegram and read it. It had been sent from Savannah.

T JARRELL 106A N BEACH DAYTONA BEACH FLA. DROVE THROUGH NIGHT. STAYING HERE TONIGHT. WILL TELEGRAM DAILY. HOWIE.

Tom smiled to himself as he put folded over the telegram and put it in his front shirt pocket. He wanted to make sure to show it to Ronnie later on.

Marveen then asked, "Did you take Mrs. Johnson's affidavit home with you last night?"

Tom looked up. "No. Why?"

Marveen's eyes widened. "It's not on my desk where I left it last night."

Tom pulled open his top drawer and pulled out the folder where he'd left the document the night before. He put it on his desk and opened it. "I showed it to Howie and then put it in here."

Marveen walked over and looked down from the side. "Oh, good," she said with a sigh of relief. She giggled a little. "I thought maybe Mr. Mayer stole it."

Tom shook his head. "He wouldn't do something like that." What he didn't say out loud was that, the night before, after Howie had read the affidavit, he'd placed the typewritten pages underneath the original shorthand notes. That was a habit of his. He liked documents to appear in a file in chronological order and, in his mind, the notes went first. When he opened the folder right then, the typewritten pages were on top. Marveen was right—they needed to change the locks.

. . .

"And, in conclusion, gentlemen, I must ask that—"

Mr. Jarrell's slow, smooth dictation was interrupted by the sudden sound of the downstairs door opening. Marveen looked up from her steno pad and watched the man's expression. He looked happy and eager, two emotions he rarely seemed to express. Once again, she had the sense that she was on the outside of something looking in. It reminded her of how she sometimes felt when she was window shopping, looking at dresses she couldn't afford and wishing she could. The feeling confused her.

The voice of Ronnie Grisham boomed up the staircase. "Tom, we have a problem."

Mr. Jarrell looked over at her and caught her watching him. He gave her that small smile of his and said, "We'll finish this up later."

She folded over her steno pad and stood. Walking back to her desk, she watched as Ronnie bounded through the outside door and strode past, completely ignoring her presence. He slammed the door to Mr. Jarrell's office. She could then hear the two of them whispering.

She dropped her pad on her desk and reached down for her purse. If the two of them wanted to be alone, she was more than happy to let them. It was a beautiful day out there and she wouldn't mind a walk along the river.

. . .

Tom had that deep crease in his forehead as he asked, "What's wrong?" He was whispering, something that, after last night, really got Ronnie's gears going.

Resisting the temptation to walk around and kiss him right on the forehead, Ronnie plopped down in the closest chair and put his shoes up on the desk. Whispering, he asked, "Did you see Mayer this morning?"

Tom nodded, his frown getting deeper. "He was here this morning when Marveen arrived. He let himself in. We need to change the locks."

"That's not all we need to do. You need to go find the judge and file that affidavit. Someone is going around town telling everyone you paid Inez Johnson to head back to New York City."

Tom sat up, his eyes bugging out. "What?"

Nodding, Ronnie said, "I just heard it from Bill Saunders."

"Is that where you went this morning?" asked Tom.

Ronnie had the feeling Tom was a little jealous. That made him grin. But, then again, it didn't take much to make him grin. He was a grinnin' fool and didn't care who liked it or didn't like it. Ronnie said, "Yes, I had some papers to get signed in Edgewater for Bill and then dropped off by his office to let him know it was done. That's where I heard all about it."

Tom nodded absentmindedly. Ronnie was pretty sure he could see the wheels of his pal's mind turning.

"Well, boy, are you gonna get goin'?"

Tom didn't say anything. Finally, he pushed a folder on his desk towards Ronnie. "Mayer read this."

Pulling his big shoes off the desk, Ronnie leaned forward and looked at the typewritten document. "How do you know?"

"The steno notes were on top when I put the folder in my desk after Howie read the affidavit yesterday."

"Are you sure?"

Tom nodded. "Definitely."

Ronnie stood. He wanted Tom to get up and take care of business. "Well?"

Tom slowly nodded and stood. "I just need Marveen to type another copy before I file this original."

Ronnie frowned. "Didn't she make a carbon copy?"

Tom looked up, the crease in his forehead as deep as Ronnie had ever seen it. "No. I told her I prefer for her to make two typewritten sets. One for signature and one for the file."

For as smart as he was, Ronnie couldn't believe how stupid his pal could be sometimes. He thought for a moment and then had an idea. He snapped his fingers. "Hold on a moment."

He took one long stride towards the office door and pulled it open. As soon as he did, he saw that Marveen was gone. She'd put the cover over her typewriter. Over his shoulder, he said, "We're down a secretary."

...

Tom walked around his desk to see what Ronnie was talking about. Sure enough, Marveen was gone. She'd put the cover over her typewriter and was nowhere to be seen. He wondered why she'd left without saying anything. Before he could figure that out, Ronnie suddenly emerged from his office with his camera in hand.

"What's that for?" asked Tom, feeling overwhelmed by the recent turn of events.

Grinning, of course, his friend replied, "Poor man's photostat."

Tom didn't understand and said as much.

Walking up, Ronnie said, "I'll take a photograph of each page and then you'll have a copy of what you're gonna submit to the court." He suddenly leaned forward and gave Tom a kiss on the lips. "Sorry," he said with a wicked grin. "Can't help it."

Tom sighed. "Now's not the time."

Looking slightly disappointed, Ronnie nodded and walked into the office. As Tom watched, he cleared a space on the desk and took the first page, turned it on its side, and carefully took a photograph.

"Why on the side?" asked Tom as he walked up next to his friend.

Turning to look at him, Ronnie replied, "Matches the size of the film."

Tom reached over and, placing his hand over Ronnie's, said, "Sorry about that a moment ago. And thanks for your help with all this."

Ronnie grinned at him and kissed him on the nose. "You're welcome." He turned back to the task at hand and began to photograph each page of the affidavit.

Tom watched him do that for a moment and then decided he needed to find out where Judge Frederick was. He figured the man was in DeLand, at the county court house, but he thought he would call and find out.

Walking over to Marveen's desk, he picked up the receiver and waited. After a moment, he heard a female voice say, "Number, please."

"Can you get me Judge Frederick's office over on Halifax?"

"One moment."

Tom heard some pages turning and then the voice asked, "Do you mean his home number? I have him listed in Port Orange."

"No, ma'am. His work number here in town. It's on Halifax by the fire station." He added, "In Daytona Beach."

"Thank you. One moment and I'll connect you."

Tom heard a click or two and then the line began to ring. On the third ring, another female voice said, "Judge Frederick's office. May I help you?"

"Is the judge in today?"

"Who's calling, please?"

"This is Thomas Jarrell."

"Hold on a moment, Mr. Jarrell."

He heard another click and then nothing. He turned and watched Ronnie place his camera on the desk and then neatly reassemble the stack of pages he'd been photographing.

The voice returned. "Judge Frederick will be here for another fifteen minutes before he has a luncheon appointment."

"Thank you. Will you let him know I'm on my way?"

"I certainly will, Mr. Jarrell," replied the voice in crisp tones.

Chapter 2

Crossing the Main Street bridge
Wednesday, September 24, 1947
A few minutes before noon

Ronnie glanced over at Tom and said, "I kinda like this, you and me, out workin' together."

His pal didn't say anything. He was looking out the passenger window at the river.

"You hear me, boy?"

Tom nodded but didn't reply.

Ronnie kept his eyes on the road and wondered if Tom was worried about the rumors flying around town. Ronnie had heard three at Bill Saunders's office but had only repeated one of them. He figured the one about how everyone was sayin' Tom had paid for Inez Johnson to leave town was more than enough.

But Bill had also mentioned how he'd heard that Howie Kirkpatrick had skipped town after being fired over at Haynes Construction. That much was true, of course, but Bill had added Howie was seen crying in the rain the day before and how it was on account of how much he missed Skipper. Ronnie had done his best to put an end to that one by telling Bill that the kid wasn't crying—he was trying to fix his old, beat-up Ford, for chrissakes. Besides, how could anyone tell if someone was crying in the middle of a tropical storm?

The third rumor Bill had asked about was if it was true that Marveen was seeing another Bill (the bum lawyer had thought that was real funny), Bill Gordon. Bill Saunders, the lawyer, was about 55 and a fat slob. Ronnie didn't say so, but Bill Gordon, the cop, was handsome enough, even if he was short enough to fit in Ronnie's pocket. And, Ronnie felt a huge amount of relief that Marveen, a nice enough gal he'd dated earlier that year, had found a man who would love her for being a woman and pretty, to boot. To answer Bill Saunders, Ronnie had said it was true and that, even though he was a little crushed that she was interested in someone else, he was happy for her and hoped it all worked out. The lawyer had grunted and then handed over the twenty bucks he owed Ronnie for his time that morning.

As he made a left on Halifax, Ronnie heard Tom sigh. "What's goin' on there, buddy?"

Turning his head back towards the windshield, Tom said, "I didn't tell you, but Mr. Mayer offered me that job again this morning."

Ronnie whistled. "Did you turn down a guaranteed ten grand a year? Again?"

Tom nodded. "I did and I think you were right last night."

Ronnie put his right hand on Tom's bony thigh. "I was right about a lot of things last night. Which one thing are you referrin' to?"

Tom pulled his pack of Pall Mall out of his coat pocket and lit one up. "About Mayer wanting me to work for him because he thinks I'm his enemy."

Ronnie reached over, pulled the cigarette out of Tom's mouth and took a quick drag on it.

Tom sighed again and then took the cigarette out of Ronnie's outstretched hand.

"Well, it's better to know where you stand."

Tom exhaled. "I know. But, there was a time when I looked up to Mr. Mayer."

Ronnie guffawed. "He's awfully short for you to try and do that."

"I'm serious, Ronnie. He taught me a lot about the business. Now I feel like I'm all alone and don't have anyone in town who can help me out when I'm not sure what to do."

Ronnie thought about that for a moment and then he realized the fire house was in the next block. He stuck his left arm out the window to let the truck that was riding his tail know he was about to turn left.

...

Judge Frederick took his time reading the affidavit. Tom didn't realize until right then that the judge used a pair of wire-rimmed spectacles to read. He'd never seen Judge Frederick using them in court.

From across the judge's desk, Tom watched the man's cheeks closely. He knew, from experience, that they flushed in spots whenever he was upset by something. As he read the second-to-the-last page, one spot appeared on his right cheek. Tom guessed the judge had just read the part where Mrs. Johnson described how her husband had taken their son, Skipper, out on the ocean and killed the young man.

Sighing, the judge nodded, as if to himself, carefully took off his glasses, and looked up at Tom. "Well, Mr. Jarrell, this is rather damning, wouldn't you say?"

"Yes, sir."

"How did you go about obtaining it?"

"Mrs. Johnson walked into my office and offered."

"In the pouring rain?" asked the judge, his head tilted skeptically to the side.

"Yes, sir."

The judge looked at his watch and said, "Well, I'm late for an appointment, so I'll have to deal with this later." He stood.

Tom did the same.

"Go back to your office and, in the matter of State versus Leland Johnson, prepare a short *amicus curiae* brief..." He walked around his desk and removed his coat from a hook on the wall. As he pulled it on, he looked at Tom. "Have you ever prepared one before?"

"Yes, sir." Tom paused and then added, "But not in this jurisdiction."

The judge put on his hat. "Where?"

"In the Southern District of New York, for one."

"Federal court?"

"Yes, sir. During my time in the Judge Advocate General's Corps in the Army."

The judge stood and looked at him. "What did you ever do to Eugene Mayer?"

Tom stepped back, surprised. "I'm not sure—"

"Well, whatever you did, he's hoppin' mad at you or so I heard this morning."

"I didn't take a job he offered me."

The judge nodded and walked into his outer office. His secretary was gone, having popped her head in earlier letting them know she was headed to lunch. "Well, that would do it. Eugene Mayer wants what he wants when he wants it." The judge put his hand on the outside door and then paused. "Didn't you attend Stetson for law school?"

"Yes, sir."

"Who was your favorite professor over there?"

"Wilkins, sir."

The judge smiled. "Good. I like ole Jedediah." He looked up at Tom. "And I like you, too, Mr. Jarrell. I was very impressed with you in court this week."

Tom blushed without meaning to. "Thank you, Your Honor."

The judge's smile broadened. "Save that for the court room and for chambers. Look," he said as he patted Tom's arm. "Why don't you head over to DeLand and have a talk with Jed Wilkins? Tell him I sent you and that I would consider it a personal favor if he would help you out with this amicus brief and..." He winked. "Anything else that you might otherwise have gone to Eugene Mayer for help with."

Chapter 3

On the DeLand Highway
Wednesday, September 24, 1947
A few minutes past 1 in the afternoon

"Do you have any idea where the place is?" asked Ronnie as he worked at keeping the car on the road. As if from out of nowhere, the wind had kicked up and was blowing Tom's Buick around the road a bit.

"The judge said they moved the law school out to the airport. I don't know where, exactly, but it shouldn't be that hard to find." He paused and then added, "Howie sent a telegram this morning from Savannah."

Ronnie whistled. "That was fast. Everything OK?"

"Sounded like it. He mentioned he was keeping his promise to send us one every day."

Ronnie nodded. "He's a good kid."

"He sure is," said Tom.

Ronnie burped. "Sorry 'bout that. I shouldn't have

had onions on my burger back at lunch. They always repeat on me." He burped again.

Out of the corner of his eye, he saw Tom look over at him and smile. "You know, you always say that every time you have onions on anything. But you always have onions."

Ronnie grinned. He wanted to reach over and put his hand on Tom's face and pull his pal in close, but he had to keep both hands on the wheel to make sure they stayed on the road. He glanced over and quickly winked at Tom, who blushed.

Neither man said anything for a moment. Then Ronnie asked, "Is that why you love me?"

Tom stiffened, or so Ronnie thought.

. . .

"Is that why you love me?"

Tom could barely believe what he was hearing. How could Ronnie ask him a question like that at a time like this? Tom was doing the best he could to hold his reputation together. Witness tampering was a serious offense and he was looking at serious prison time if he was convicted on the hearsay rumors floating around town that he'd sent Inez Johnson back to New York by bribing her, or whatever they were saying.

He had enough to think about without worrying what Ronnie was going to do next. His friend had always been impulsive. That was what made him so attractive, besides the fact that he was handsome, in an odd sort of way, and was thickly built with plenty of muscles popping out everywhere, something Tom always found attractive in a man.

Staring out at the ribbon of highway that was passing below them in the wind-blown car, Tom thought about their time together the night before and how passionate things had been. That was another thing that attracted him to Ronnie. The man was relaxed when it came to carnal matters. He was friendly and passionate and gentle, while also being driven and almost single-minded in his desire to know that Tom was enjoying himself. It had always been that way.

In the few encounters of a similar nature that Tom had during his time in the Army, he'd been shocked at how selfish other men could be. They seemed to want to be satisfied but had no interest in the sort of quiet conversation intermingled with passionate lovemaking that Tom had always loved having with Ronnie and Sarah, both.

Sarah.

What would she think if she knew what they got up to in the bed she had slept in before she died? Would she be repelled? Disgusted?

Ronnie claimed that she had given her blessing to their fooling around. And, on those nights when she wasn't home, having taken Missy over to the Gulf Coast to spend a few days with relatives who didn't like Tom, he and Ronnie would fool around in that bed. But they had never slept together. And Tom had always made sure to change the sheets before Sarah got home.

He couldn't really imagine the conversation she had with Ronnie about all that. He'd claimed that she'd invited him over for dinner and, while drinking beer, had admitted she knew all about how they felt about each other. He even claimed, Ronnie had, that she had blessed their fooling around.

Tom sighed. He wavered back and forth about whether to believe Ronnie on that score. It seemed both highly unlikely and exactly what Sarah would have done. There had been a number of occasions, during their marriage, when she had kindly sat down with him and told him she knew what he was up to and it didn't bother her at all. He couldn't remember the specific things—they had all been small, household sorts of things—but he could easily picture her open and frank expression as she looked right at Ronnie and said something like, *"I know you're in love with Tom as much as I am."*

The sudden intensity of that thought shocked him. Of course she had said that to Ronnie. He didn't know how he knew, but he did. He could feel in it his bones. Over the sound of the tires on the road and the slight moaning of the wind as it buffeted the car around, he could hear her next sentence, *"And I know Tom loves you in a way he could never love me."*

That thought made him jump in his seat.

"You OK, buddy?"

Ronnie's voice brought him suddenly back to the present. He turned and, not understanding the reason the words seemed so obvious, he said, "I love you Ronnie and I always have. Ever since the first day I met you in high school."

. . .

Ronnie grinned when he heard Tom say that. But, then again, he always grinned. He was a grinnin' fool. But he loved Tom, too, and he always had.

They'd both been 17 when they met. Until Ronnie's mother died, he'd always lived in the same four-room house on the north side of Tuscaloosa, up in Alabama. Then she stepped on a rusty nail one day and died, a week later, from lockjaw. His old man never recovered from it. Trying to make a new life for the two of them, his father had moved them moved to Birmingham and then Jackson, Mississippi, and then Mobile and, finally, Tallahassee.

Ronnie and Tom met in the hallway of Leon High School, back when it was in the old building on Park Avenue. Ronnie was already standing at 6'5", as tall as he would ever get, and skinny as a rail (but not for long). Tom was still a short little runt, barely coming up to his shoulder. But then he got his massive growth spurt in the fall and over Christmas and, by the time they graduated, they could look at each other right in the eyes.

Ronnie's old man went to sleep one night, stone drunk, and choked on his own vomit. That was in April of 1935, a few weeks before graduation. Tom's parents had, without hesitation, brought Ronnie into their home and set up a second single bed in Tom's room on the second floor, behind the bathroom and far away from Mr. and Mrs. Jarrell's room. One thing had led to another and, by graduation day, Ronnie considered himself practically married to Tom.

As he held onto the wheel to keep the car straight, he thought about that first day at Leon High. Being the tallest kid in the school had its advantages. He could see everyone in the hallways, for one thing. He had to sit in the last row of the classroom so he could stretch his legs. It made him popular with the girls, of course, even as gangly as he was at the time. And, it gave him a chance to take a look at all the boys who were watching the girls who were watching him.

And, on that first day at Leon High, he'd been loping down the hall, headed to his English classroom (something he already knew, on the first day, he would barely pass), when he bumped into a kid barreling out of a classroom. Both their books went flying and, as they scrambled to pick things up, Ronnie had taken a moment to get a good look at the kid he'd hit. Suddenly aware that the kid wasn't some pipsqueak sophomore, but a senior, Ronnie found it hard to speak. Tom wasn't particularly handsome. He was painfully thin and obviously shy. But there was something in his eyes that Ronnie couldn't stop staring at. He knew from the get-go that Tom was probably the smartest kid he would ever meet. And, over time, that turned out to be more true than Ronnie would have ever thought possible.

...

Tom pointed at the sign for the airport. "There it is."

"Way ahead of you," replied Ronnie.

That was the first time either of them had spoken since Tom had clumsily made his declaration of love. He was embarrassed for having done so, particularly since, in the silence that followed, he was wondering if Ronnie didn't love him as much or if he just wanted him around for... *For what?*

Before he could think about that too much, Ronnie asked, "Mind if I drop you off here?"

"No," replied Tom, suddenly convinced he was right. Ronnie was just using him. He was using Tom's car and dropping Tom off at the law school and then off to do some other job for another lawyer. He suddenly felt jealous.

Ronnie added, "I need to take care of a quick job for Bill Saunders at the courthouse."

Tom nodded tersely. "Fine. This might take an hour or so."

Ronnie didn't reply to that. He pulled over to the curb next to a big building that reminded Tom of a gymnasium. According to its sign, however, it was the administration hall for the law school.

Tom got out and then opened the back door, reached for his briefcase, and slammed the door closed as he quickly walked into the building without saying anything. Behind him, he heard the car squeal out.

...

Jed Wilkins looked just like he had when Tom last saw him the day he graduated from the law school in 1942. He was, maybe, a little thinner, but his wild white hair was still sticking out in every direction and Tom was pretty sure he was wearing the same blue and brown cardigan sweater he'd worn on that day. Tom and his classmates had, over the three years they'd studied and worked together, catalogued Wilkins's entire wardrobe, which consisted of four shirts, five cardigan sweaters, three pairs of trousers, and two hats. The hats could barely contain the hair and mostly sat atop it.

Wilkins (among other degrees, he had a Ph.D. in history from Columbia University in New York, but refused to be called mister, doctor or, even, professor) looked up as Tom entered his makeshift office. The man's dull brown eyes widened with surprise and then he smiled. "Thomas Jarrell." He stood and offered his hand which Tom quickly shook.

"Hello, Wilkins. How are you?"

"Fine, Jarrell." He pointed to the one empty chair in the cluttered office. "Have a seat."

Tom did just that, putting his briefcase on the floor to the right of the chair.

"How are you?"

Tom smiled as much as he could considering he was still smarting from the ride over from Daytona Beach in the car with Ronnie, and said, "Just fine. Thank you, sir."

The man across the desk scowled. "None of that."

Tom's smile widened. "Sorry. Judge Frederick sent me over."

Wilkins tilted his head. "That so?"

"Yes. I need to file an amicus brief in his court and he suggested I come talk to you about the form to use."

Wilkins folded his hands on the desk, a move that reminded Tom of several long conversations in the man's old office in Elizabeth Hall over at the main campus. "Well, I'm an instructor in the law, not a practitioner, as Frederick knows as well as anyone else. I'd suggest you go see Jordan in DeLand. His daughter is our librarian." He tilted his head again. "She's single."

Tom smiled again, this time to hide his embarrassment at the subject being brought up.

As if realizing what he'd just done, Jenkins frowned. "My apologies, Jarrell. I was very sorry to hear about Sarah and Missy."

Tom nodded. "Thank you. She really liked you."

"That so?"

"Sarah liked anyone who was direct and straightforward."

Laughing, Jenkins said, "She never would have made a good clubwoman, is that what you mean?"

Tom nodded, suddenly awash with grief for Sarah. He missed her smile and her small confidences and then there was Missy... Before he fell over that chasm and completely lost himself, he cleared his throat and said the next thing on his mental list. "Judge Frederick also wanted me to tell you how much he likes you." Tom blushed. That didn't come out right at all.

Jenkins leaned forward. "I can't imagine what it's like to lose your wife and your daughter, all at once. I hope you have people around you who are helping."

Tom nodded. He took another wild emotional swing and realized that Ronnie wasn't using him. Ronnie was helping him. Ronnie was, in fact, loving him. Just like he always had. Ronnie was the best man he'd ever known. He was loyal to a fault and generous and always ready to tell a joke or lighten a tense situation. Even when he was a little too much of a goof, he was always amenable to being told to cut it out. With a start, Tom realized a couple of tears had suddenly rolled down his left cheek. He pulled out his handkerchief apologetically and wiped his face.

"Nothing wrong with a tear or two, Jarrell." The other man leaned back in his chair. "I am glad to see you and was thinking of coming to see you myself."

"Oh?" asked Tom, as he put away his handkerchief.

Wilkins nodded. "I heard about your performance at the courthouse on Monday, so I sent Houseman, a second year, over on Tuesday to take notes and report back. I had a class, otherwise I would have gone myself." Wilkins reached over to a pipe rack and pulled out a modern-looking one. He opened a jar of tobacco and, with his fingers, stuffed some in the pipe's bowl. "Impressive stuff." Putting the pipe in his mouth, he pulled out a big box of matches and lit one. Tom watched, transfixed, as the man worked to light the tobacco and get a good draw on the smoke.

Once that was done, Wilkins took a long look at Tom. After getting two or three good puffs, filling the air with the spicy smell of his tobacco, he removed the pipe and pointed it at Tom. "You better watch your step."

Not sure what to say, Tom waited.

"Even here in the middle of this godforsaken airport, I hear things and word is that Eugene Mayer is on the warpath."

Tom nodded.

"Good. I'm glad you know what he's up to. My question is: Why?" Wilkins looked at Tom the same way he did when asking about a point of constitutional law, with his left eye wide open and his right eye nearly closed. It was as intimidating as ever.

"Because I didn't take a job he offered me."

Wilkins nodded. "Why did he offer you the job?"

Tom shrugged, instantly regretting doing so.

Frowning, Wilkins said, "Jarrell, you know better than that."

Tom swallowed hard, just like he had once done after shrugging when being asked by Wilkins about the meaning of the ruling in *Hans v. Louisiana*. Feeling as panicked as he had back then, he blurted out, "Because he's trying to keep his enemies close."

Wilkins smiled a little and then tilted his head again. "Are you an enemy of Eugene Mayer?"

"No." He almost added "sir" but caught himself in time. "I think he thinks I am but I'm not."

"Eugene Mayer is a snake and you'd be well-advised to give him a wide berth. Also, I'd have advised you to take the job. How much did you make before he fired you last summer?"

"Five thousand."

Wilkins grunted. "That's more than I make but, then again, I barely work at all compared to a low-level lawyer in the offices of Mayer & Thornton." He grinned and then took a puff on his pipe. "How much did he offer you this time?"

"Twice that."

Wilkins laughed. "Well, never let it be said that the man isn't smart. And, since he can't have you, he's out to destroy you." He paused for a moment. "What was the name of that young man who was such a good friend to you and Sarah?"

Tom tried to hide his surprise. "Ronnie Grisham."

Wilkins cleared his throat and looked at his pipe. "I suppose you and Grisham are now an item."

Unable to stop himself, Tom blushed as hot as he ever had. He also started sweating.

"Don't worry, Jarrell, we all have secrets." He took another puff. "Mine was Ramon Geraldo. He was Cuban and his father owned a huge sugar plantation. We met at Columbia and it was love at first sight."

Feeling a little panicked, Tom looked around. The makeshift office was one of several partitioned out of a large room that could have easily been a gymnasium when the Navy had possession of the airport during the war. The walls only went up about six and a half feet and the ceiling was another ten or so feet above that.

"Don't worry, we're all alone. Everyone else is teaching. I'm the only one here." Wilkins leaned forward. "Why not sell and move down to Miami? Or go to San Francisco and apply to the California bar?"

Tom blinked several times and replied, "I don't want to leave Daytona Beach. It feels like home."

Wilkins put his pipe in a big ashtray and folded his hands again. "Well, that's as good a reason as any. But watch your step." He tilted his head one more time. "What is this amicus brief about?"

Tom felt a little relieved to talk about the law. He wasn't sure how he felt to discover his favorite professor was an invert. For some reason, it seemed to sully the man's reputation in his own mind. Brushing that uncomfortable thought from his mind, he reached down for his briefcase. As he opened it, he asked, "Do you know the names of the parties involved in the trial?"

Wilkins smiled a little. "Leland and Inez Johnson. Their boy, Roland, a.k.a., Skipper, was the deceased. Your client was Howard Kirkpatrick, Skipper's lover, from what I hear."

Tom nodded, not liking the fact that Wilkins had used the word "lover." He wordlessly handed over the affidavit to the other man.

Wilkins quickly read the thing. Tom had forgotten the man could read twice as fast as anyone else. Looking up when he was done, Wilkins smiled. "Hot stuff."

Tom grinned at the phrase.

"Frederick wants you to submit this as an amicus brief in the case of State versus Leland Johnson?"

"Yes."

"That must mean that Johnson, the elder, is going to plead not guilty."

Tom hadn't thought of that.

"When is arraignment?"

"I don't know. It wasn't today. Judge Frederick was in Daytona."

Wilkins nodded thoughtfully. "You do realize that if you file this brief and Inez Johnson isn't called, you very well might be. Mayer may try to impeach your credibility. He's already saying you paid her to leave town."

Tom nodded. "Yes. I've thought of that."

Handing the document back, Wilkins asked, "Are you still going to file it?"

Tom frowned slightly. "Of course. I'm an officer of the court."

Wilkins nodded enigmatically. "Yes, Jarrell, you certainly are."

Chapter 4

Driving into DeLand
Wednesday, September 24, 1947
Later that afternoon

"Did you get the job done for Saunders?" asked Tom.

Ronnie nodded, still driving. "It wasn't much. He just wanted me to check something with the clerk."

Tom was torn. As much as he knew he had no right to ask, he was curious to know what Ronnie was up to. But, unlike earlier, he was no longer jealous. He was simply curious. "Do you mind me asking about your other jobs?"

Ronnie glanced over at him. He looked serious, which was rare. "No. But there's something I want to talk to you about."

Tom braced himself. "What?"

"How about if you put me on a minimum retainer so I wouldn't have to take on these other jobs? I think it could get real sticky, otherwise."

Tom breathed out a sigh of relief. He even laughed.

"What's so funny?"

"Nothing, really. And, yes, I'd be happy to do that. How about 75 dollars a week?"

Ronnie nodded. "That's more than fair. I'll still bill you my usual rate plus expenses."

"Of course. When we get back to the office, I'll tell Marveen to set that up. And I'll deduct the first 75 of your billing to compensate for the retainer. We'll handle it like that."

"Sounds good," said Ronnie. He looked over at Tom as they drove by the main campus of Stetson, headed south towards downtown. "There's something I wanna tell you."

Tom braced himself again. "What's that?"

"I love you, too, and I always have and always will."

Tom breathed out a bigger sigh of relief. He put his left hand on Ronnie's thick right thigh and left it there until they were parked in front of Ray Jordan's office on New York Avenue.

. . .

"Well, Mr. Jarrell, you certainly made quite a splash yesterday, no doubt about it." Ray Jordan was a slim man with hair that was thinning on top. He wore steel-framed glasses that reminded Tom of President Truman.

"Thanks for seeing me on such short notice, Mr. Jordan."

The man sat back in his big leather chair. "Call me, Ray."

Tom smiled. "Thank you, Ray. And I'm Tom."

The older man said, "So, old Wilkins sent you over, did he?"

"Yes, sir. Judge Frederick thought I might need some help with an amicus brief he wants me to file."

"Would this be in State versus Johnson?"

"Yes, sir."

Mr. Jordan leaned forward. "What's in the brief?"

"Notice of an affidavit filed by Mrs. Johnson."

With a twinkle in his eye, the other man asked, "The woman you paid to leave Daytona?"

"That's what they say."

"Well, if she's so rich, as everyone knows she was in her own right, then why does she need some country-bumpkin lawyer like yourself payin' her to get out of town?" He grinned across his desk. "No offense intended."

"None taken."

Mr. Jordan smiled and then looked around Tom towards his office door. "Wanda!"

. . .

"That should do it," said Mr. Jordan. He walked in from the outer office and handed the typewritten notice to Tom and said, "Just walk across the street and—" He laughed and patted Tom on the shoulder. "I don't need to tell you that part. I asked Wanda to type up a few other sample forms that I thought you could use. Come by and get them once you've filed this."

Tom stood and reached out his hand. "Thanks, Ray."

The older man shook and nodded. "Happy to help. Let me know if you need anything else." He paused. "And don't pay too much attention to Gene Mayer. Most everyone in this county has been bitten by him, so they know that the bullshit he's trading around Daytona is just that. Besides, like I said, Inez Johnson was just about the wealthiest woman on her own account in Daytona Beach. And, you wouldn't have enough money in the world to get her to do something she didn't want to do."

Tom thought he heard something in the other man's voice, so he asked, "Did you know Mrs. Johnson?"

Mr. Jordan screwed up his face for a moment. "I did some work for her, nothing I can talk about, of course, but there were times when it was helpful for her to have her own lawyer." He paused and then added, "Particularly one outside of Daytona Beach." He slapped Tom on the back. "Better go file your mysterious affidavit." He followed Tom into the outer office. "I'd really like to know what it says, but I specifically didn't ask you about it because it's none of my beeswax."

. . .

Ronnie looked over at Tom. "So, what's next?" They were sitting across from each other in a small coffee shop called The Sugar Bowl on Woodland. While Ronnie had waited in the car, Tom had filed the amicus brief, stopped back in at Mr. Jordan's office, and picked up the sample forms Wanda had typed up for him. After that, the two of them had walked the couple of blocks up Woodland to the little diner.

Tom's forehead creased a little. Ronnie resisted the temptation to reach over and kiss it. "Now that's all done, I'm worried about Marveen."

Ronnie grinned. "I called her while you were in with Jordan. She said she just needed to stretch her legs."

"Did she sound upset?"

"Not particularly, why?"

Ronnie watched as Tom looked down at his cup of coffee. "I lied to her the other day."

Reaching into his shirt pocket, Ronnie pulled out his pack of Lucky Strikes. He offered one to Tom, who shook his head, and then lit one up for himself. Exhaling to the side, he asked, "What'd you say to her?"

That crease deepened. "She said she couldn't figure out what was going on in the office and I knew what she meant but I pretended there was nothing to it." He looked at Ronnie dead in the eye.

"Yeah. She's smart. It's just a matter of time before she figures it out." He took a deep drag on his cigarette and watched Tom closely.

"Well, what do we do?"

Ronnie grinned and exhaled to his side again. "Let her come to you. She won't talk to me about it."

Tom nodded and looked at his coffee again. "Do you think she'll quit?"

"Hell, no," said Ronnie with a chuckle.

Looking up, Tom asked, "Why do you say that?"

Ronnie wasn't sure why he knew, but he did. He figured Marveen for a broad-minded kind of gal. He hoped he was right. If not, things could go south pretty damn quick and he and Tom might find themselves running from a mob, trying to get out while the getting was good.

"Well?" asked Tom.

"Well, boy, there's always Miami or New York City."

Tom smiled a little. It was hard not to reach over and kiss those lips, but Ronnie managed not to do so. "Wilkins said the same thing."

"Professor Wilkins?"

Nodding with a sigh, Tom said, "He admitted he's, you know..."

Ronnie leaned back, took a last, long drag on his Lucky Strike, and then stubbed it out in the ashtray by the napkin dispenser on the table. "Well, ain't that a kick in the ass?"

Tom looked confused. "What do you mean?"

Ronnie took a sip from his coffee and then tried to decide whether to say why he was so amused by that news. Putting a toe in what might be some rough waters, he asked, "Are you sure you wanna know?"

"I guess."

Ronnie grinned. "Remember when you enlisted?"

"Sure."

"And Sarah, Missy, and me saw you off at the train station over in Daytona?"

"Yes."

"Well, Sarah and Missy headed for Tampa to go see those snooty relatives of hers."

Tom nodded. "I remember that. She was going over for a few days and then, when she got back, the two of you finished packing up the house and then you moved her back to my folks' house in Tallahassee."

Ronnie nodded and took another sip of coffee. "Well, what you don't know is that after she dropped me off at my little garage apartment over on San Souci, I got all spiffed up and headed back over to Daytona for the night."

"Really?" asked Tom. It might have been Ronnie's imagination, but he thought his pal looked a little jealous. He was pretty sure he'd seen the same narrow eyes on Tom earlier when he'd dropped him off at the law school.

"Yeah. So, one thing led to another and I ended up making an unscheduled stop at a room in the Plaza."

Tom nodded tensely. Ronnie was right! Tom *was* jealous.

"And, you know, a good time was had by all. Anyway, he took me out for a steak dinner that night. He was about 40, maybe, Cuban, and from New York City."

Tom's face changed in a flash. "Did he know Wilkins?"

Ronnie nodded, enjoying the moment. He liked it when he knew something Tom didn't. It happened often enough, but it made Ronnie a little excited whenever it did. Tom was so smart that Ronnie felt like he was playing a game with his pal and had just scored.

"Well?" asked Tom.

"Well, this man, his name was Ramon, I think. He told me how he knew Wilkins and how they'd been lovers in New York City. I didn't think anything of it at the time. Every Cuban I've known was a little bit crazy."

"I don't understand."

Ronnie was confused for a moment. He replayed what he'd said in his head and then got it. "Sorry. At the time, I didn't know he was talking about Wilkins. All he would say was that he knew this important professor at Stetson and how he couldn't tell me who it was and all that."

The crease was back and deeper than ever. "I still don't understand. If he wouldn't tell you, then how do you know it was Wilkins?"

Ronnie grinned. "I put it together later on, when we were back in his room for round two and I was giving it to him good. He called me Jed. Not once, but five times."

Tom suddenly laughed and, as usual, Ronnie fell in love with his pal a little bit more as a result.

Chapter 5

106A N. Beach Street
Daytona Beach, Fla.
Wednesday, September 24, 1947
A few minutes before 5 in the afternoon

Marveen sighed and put down her book.

She was done with all the work on her desk. She'd cleaned the entire office, top to bottom. She'd made a quick trip to the A&P at the corner of Beach and Bay to buy another can of coffee and, on a whim, decided to get a box of Uneeda Biscuits and a box of Oreos. She'd then stopped in at the Walgreen's and found a couple of tin boxes to store the biscuits and the cookies in since they were in Florida. Everyone knew you couldn't leave anything like that exposed to the humid air or the little critters that might find their way to something tasty. She'd then made her way back to the office, unpacked her goodies, put everything up, nice and neat, and sat down at her desk and started her book.

It was called *Mrs. Mike*. She was only a few pages in and was wondering if the story was going anywhere. She'd picked it up at the library on Tuesday morning, expecting Mr. Jarrell would be in court all day, but he wasn't, so she'd never had a chance to read it until then and wasn't too sure about it.

She'd been attracted to the story because the new librarian (whose name she couldn't remember) had told her it was about a young girl in Canada who fell in love with a Mountie. Supposedly, it was a true tale, or close enough to one. She was secretly hoping the story would talk about what it was like to fall in love with a cop. She knew Mounties were like cops, but probably more like G-men than a beat cop, which is what Bill was even though her mother had openly wondered why he wasn't a sergeant yet. Marveen thought Bill was probably too young. He was only 26, after all.

She closed the book and put it back in her desk. She was in love with a cop. Or maybe it was just infatuation. She didn't think so because she'd barely eaten a thing in two days which was so unlike her.

Bill Gordon was so unlike any of the other men she'd ever dated. They'd been out two nights in a row. No man had ever asked her out for a second date that fast. She had a feeling he was as lonely in his life as she was in hers. Of course, she lived with her mother over on the beachside on Wild Olive. He, on the other hand, lived alone on the mainland in a garage apartment a few blocks north on Burleigh Avenue, at the corner of 3rd Street. He was from Ocala, which is where his parents, Ed and June, still lived, in the house he grew up in. They were just down the street from Bill's older brother, Robbie, who lived with his wife, Mary Sue, and their twin boys, Billy and Robbie, Jr.

When Marveen had recounted all their names that

morning over breakfast, her mother had asked, "Did he show you snapshots of them?"

Marveen had replied that he had and her mother had nodded with a cryptic smile.

She didn't know, but she was pretty sure her mother knew Bill was just as serious about things as she was.

That was ridiculous, of course. *Who falls in love that fast?* Marveen knew better than to wear her heart on her sleeve. She had once thought she was in love with Gary Young, her last boyfriend. But he had run off to Pensacola to marry a lumber heiress from Alabama, leaving her high and dry. Of course, she'd been on a few dates with Ronnie after Gary ran off, but nothing much had come from that and, for whatever reason, she was glad.

She thought about Gary, and how disappointed he'd been to discover that, although he was distantly related to the Dodge family of Michigan, her father had not been a wealthy man, by any means. He'd died the summer after she'd graduated from Seabreeze High. He'd left a small pension, a life insurance policy, and a house that was paid off, but she and her mother were not rich by any stretch.

In stark contrast, Bill wanted to hear everything she could tell him about her father. Hadn't he been a sergeant for the Daytona Beach police when he'd died? Bill told her that Chief Johnson still talked fondly of him and how he'd always admired her father's picture on the wall in the cramped station on Magnolia on the far side of the train tracks.

Her mother was of the opinion that Marveen was in love with a cop because her father had been a cop. She was also of the opinion that Marveen should be careful not to say, "cop," to Bill. In all fairness, she did remember how much her father hated that word... Well, hate wasn't probably the right way to describe it. In any event, he didn't like the word, that was for certain.

But Bill used the word. He called himself a cop, and proudly, or so Marveen thought.

She sighed again, as she thought of their date the night before. The Trocadero was a bit of a racy spot. It was at the Riviera Hotel up just south of Ormond and real nice. Bill had treated her to dinner, including a shrimp cocktail as an appetizer. She'd even had two rum cocktails, something she rarely did. They'd danced until midnight and then he'd slowly driven her home, stopping to park for a little while in a dark spot just outside Holly Hill. He told her that he knew the local deputy sheriff, Dick Noonan, never looked at that spot twice on his rounds.

Still, she was a little afraid someone might see them and think she was a fast girl, but then her mother had reminded her over breakfast that parking, these days, was as much a part of getting to know someone as swapping snapshots of family members could be.

Marveen let her feet tap a little as she hummed the one song she'd loved the most last night. "If I Could Be With You" really stuck with her and she'd loved how closely Bill had held her as the band had played, slowing it down nicely. Of course, she'd heard all sorts of stories about the Trocadero and the Riviera. One girl she knew at Seabreeze High, Maybell McMahon (what a name!), had claimed that she'd once found two men dancing (together!) and kissing out along the promenade that led down to the river. She'd been out late with her parents and decided to have a look at the river by moonlight and had received the shock of her life when she'd stumbled across the scene.

For some reason, that made Marveen think about Ronnie and Mr. Jarrell. She'd talked to Ronnie earlier that afternoon and had decided to wait until 5 on the dot for the two of them to get back from DeLand before she packed up and left for the day. Over the phone, he'd asked her if she'd been upset earlier and she'd breezily lied and said she only needed to stretch her legs. She still wasn't sure what it was that was going on in the office that made her so uncomfortable, but she'd resolved not to just walk out again. Mother always said it was important to look trouble in the eye and not back down. The next time she felt that queer sensation that they were hiding something, and for no good reason, she would just walk right into Mr. Jarrell's office and tell him she wanted to know what the big secret was, or she was leaving!

She looked at her watch. It was a minute past 5 and she was ready to go. So, she did, carefully locking the downstairs door on her way out.

Chapter 6

106A N. Beach Street
Daytona Beach, Fla.
Thursday, September 25, 1947
Half past 9 in the morning

Tom sighed. He was looking at three identical letters he'd received from the Allied Southern Insurance company of Nashville. They were from a lawyer, a man by the name of Milton P. Runnels, III. And they were each a very polite refusal to pay off three valid life insurance claims.

As he paged through each letter, he realized they looked and read the same. He placed each one on his desk, side-by-side, and saw they were, in fact, precisely identical—all the line breaks in the paragraphs, the wording of each paragraph, and, most importantly, the reasoning for the rejection. In each instance, Mr. Runnels was claiming that each insured had failed to make their monthly policy payments in a timely manner. No proof was offered, however.

Tom sat back and wondered if there really was such a person as Milton P. Runnels, III. He held up the first letter to the sunlight streaming in through the window overlooking Beach Street. If he wasn't mistaken, the signature was from a block stamp cleverly constructed to resemble one made with an ink pen.

He was about to call in Ronnie for a second opinion when Marveen knocked on the door frame.

"Mr. Jarrell?" She looked and sounded upset.

He smiled, wondering if she was finally going to bring up what was going on between Ronnie and him. "Yes, Marveen?"

"Here's a telegram from Howie."

He looked up as she handed it to him. "I didn't hear the boy from Western Union."

She nodded but didn't smile.

He opened the envelope and pulled out the telegram. It was from Savannah like the one from the day before:

T JARRELL 106A N BEACH DAYTONA BEACH FLA. STILL HERE. MAYBE ONE MORE DAY THEN GOING NORTH. HOWIE.

Taking a deep breath, Marveen asked, "Do you have a minute?"

He nodded, folded over the telegram, and put it in his shirt pocket to show Ronnie later when they went to lunch. "Of course. Have a seat."

She quietly closed the door and took a seat. He noticed she was sitting on the edge and perfectly erect.

"What can I do for you?"

She took another deep breath and said, "I'm not sure how to say this, but—"

Right then, Tom heard someone knocking on the exterior door.

Marveen rolled her eyes, stood, and went to let them in, whoever it was.

. . .

It was Volusia County Sheriff's Deputy Jesse Good. And he looked nervous as he stood in the office next to Marveen's desk and looked up at Tom. "Are you Thomas Jarrell?"

Tom smiled. "Of course, Jesse." He chuckled, amused at the freckle-faced deputy's formal tone. "You must have a subpoena."

Deputy Good nodded. His pale face flushed suddenly as he handed an envelope to Tom. As if reciting a poem in front of his high school English class, he said, "You have been served. You are to appear before Judge Herbert Frederick in DeLand in Circuit Court at 10 a.m. on Monday, September 29th, in the matter of State of Florida versus Leland Johnson." He hesitated and frowned. After a moment, he pulled a card from his pocket and then read from that. "Should you fail to appear, you will be held in contempt of court and may be subject to a fine or jail time. Do you understand?"

Tom's smile had faded by then. He said, "I do," and proceeded to open the envelope and look at the final sheet of the three-page subpoena. It was signed by Eugene Mayer. Looking over at Deputy Good, he asked, "Did Mayer tell you to use the whole form?"

The deputy nodded. He put the card back in his shirt pocket and, taking out his handkerchief and wiping his face, he replied, "Yes, sir. And he was real particular about it. Even had his secretary type it out for me and everything." He sighed. "I just came from there, in fact. He called Sherriff Littlefield and demanded I deliver this myself." He looked around as if someone might be listening in. In a whisper, he added, "I know what he's been saying about you around the county and believe me, Mr. Jarrell, no one is paying any mind to him whatsoever."

Tom smiled. "Thanks, Jesse. Do you need me to sign anything?"

Stuffing his big, white handkerchief into his front trouser pocket, the deputy shook his head. "No, sir." Tipping his hat towards Marveen, he said, "Thank you, Marveen." He looked back at Tom. "Y'all have a good day, ya hear?"

All Tom could get out was, "You too, Jesse," before the deputy was out the door and scrambling down the stairs.

Ronnie, who had been watching from just outside his office door, asked, "Well, what's it say?"

Tom quickly read it to himself and then replied, "Not much. Just the usual legal stuff and a demand to bring anything related to Inez Johnson's affidavit." He looked down at Marveen. "I'll need your steno notes." To Ronnie, he added, "And those photographs you took of the pages I filed yesterday."

Ronnie nodded. "I'm headin' over to T.J.'s place here in a bit to get him to develop the film." He looked at Tom. "You want me to put the negatives somewhere safe?"

Even though he wasn't concerned, Tom nodded. "Do you have a safety deposit box?"

Ronnie grinned. "I do. It's at Fidelity Trust, owned by Leland Johnson, current murder defendant."

Tom laughed and then looked down at Marveen who was not amused.

...

Marveen looked at her watch. She was antsy and for no good reason. It was half past 10 and too early for lunch. Then she remembered the Oreo cookies she'd bought the day before and stood up to take out a couple to have with a refill of coffee.

Once that was done, she settled back in behind her desk with three cookies on her steno pad and a fresh cup of coffee next to that and wondered what she should do next. She was glad, in a way, that her conversation with Mr. Jarrell had been interrupted. After all, her mother had said—

"Marveen?"

She jumped a little and looked up at Mr. Jarrell who was looming over her. With the bright light coming in through the window that looked out at the river, he seemed to be in shadow. Smoothing out her dress, she said, "Yes, sir?"

"I'm sorry we were interrupted earlier. Do you still want to talk?"

Marveen tried to decide. While she did that, Mr. Jarrell pulled over a chair and sat next to her desk. That put her more at ease, so she said, "Well, it's like this, Mr. Jarrell." She took in a deep breath and continued. "I don't know how to ask you this question since it's none of my business, really." She paused. Her mother had told her to be direct and not to worry about being fired. After all, Mr. Jarrell had a lot more to lose than Marveen did.

"What's that?" asked Mr. Jarrell. Again, with his back to the window, she couldn't see his face very well, so she wasn't sure what his expression might be. His voice sounded a little worried, but she wasn't sure.

"Well, I had a long talk with Mother last night about a few things that have been bothering me." She took another deep breath.

"Yes?"

She really wished he would just stay quiet and let her get through what she needed to get through. Taking yet another deep breath, she said, "And, well, she suggested I talk with you about what I think is going on here that I don't quite understand." Suddenly, the words rushed out of her. "I've been feeling like a stranger looking in from the outside, like I'm window shopping and seeing expensive dresses I like a lot but couldn't possibly afford and, well, it really gets to me sometimes and Mother thinks I should talk to you about it but, to be honest, it's confusing but, then again, it's none of my business but do you think it's possible that you and Ronnie are in love?" She gasped at the end when the words finally came out.

Mr. Jarrell crossed his arms and didn't say anything immediately.

Since she couldn't see his face, she had no idea what he might be thinking, so she said, "I told Mother this was not a good idea and I'm so sorry if I just offended you. I'm not accusing you of anything, but I don't like how confusing this all is and I really do like you a lot. You're the best boss I've ever had, and I know when things pick up that we'll have lots of work and I don't want to leave."

Mr. Jarrell nodded. "I don't want you to leave, either."

Marveen sighed with relief. "You don't?"

"No, I don't. Your work is good and you're doing a great job of keeping the office clean." He stopped for a moment. "Are there any more of those cookies?"

Happy to have something to do, Marveen stood and walked over to the cupboard where she'd put the tins the day before. "Oh, sure. I bought some Oreos and some Uneeda Biscuits. Which would you like?"

"I'll take a couple of Oreos, thanks."
"How about some coffee?"
"No, thanks."
Using the one saucer they had on hand, Marveen put two of the black cookies with white cream centers on it and walked over to Mr. Jarrell.
As he took the saucer, he said, "Thanks. Maybe we need some plates and things like that for when we eat in the office."
Marveen sat back at her desk. "Oh, sure."
Mr. Jarrell popped an entire cookie in his mouth and quickly chewed and swallowed it. "But then we would need a sink for the dishes, don't you think?"
Marveen looked over at the little counter Ronnie had built for the percolator. The cupboard was above that. Turning back to Mr. Jarrell, she said, "There must be plumbing in that wall. The bathroom is behind there."
Mr. Jarrell popped the second Oreo in his mouth and quickly ate it as well. Handing the saucer back to Marveen, he said, "That's easy enough. And, the next time you're out, could you pick up a box of Lorna Doones?" He sighed. "Those were Missy's favorites and I'm partial to them, myself."
At the mention of Missy's name, Marveen immediately wished she'd kept her big mouth shut. Mr. Jarrell had enough to deal with without her coming into the office and demanding the details of his personal life that really were none of her business. She was gonna give her mother a piece of her mind when she got home. If only—
"And maybe a box of ginger snaps?" continued Mr. Jarrell. "Those are Ronnie's favorites and, yes, Marveen, I'm in love with him."

. . .

"Well, long time no see, Mr. Ronnie Grisham."

Ronnie grinned as he held out his hand. "How are you, T.J.?"

"Oh, I'm fair to fair. How 'bout yerself?"

Ronnie reached into his coat pocket and pulled out a canister of film. "Fine. Do you think you could develop this for me today?"

T.J. palmed the cannister and then placed it on the counter in front of him. "Sure. It's not girlie nudes or nothin' like that, is it?"

Ronnie laughed. "Not this time."

"Good. Chief Johnson's been breathin' down my neck again about indecency ever since Brother Chisholm got busted back in August."

Ronnie propped his right elbow on the photo shop counter and leaned on it. "You know, I never heard what happened with ole Brother Chisholm."

T.J. took out a pack of Camels from his shirt pocket and offered it to Ronnie, who took one himself. Lighting up his first, T.J. held out his lighter so that Ronnie could lean down and light his own. Once that was done, T.J. sucked hard on his Camel and then exhaled. Blue smoke filled the small front area of the camera shop. "Well, you know that Brother Chisholm was one of those snake handlin' preachers, right?"

Ronnie exhaled. "Sure. Wasn't he from North Carolina?"

"Tennessee."

"Same difference."

T.J. grinned, showing his perfectly straight and perfectly yellow set of choppers. "Well, anyhow, seems like one of his parishioners, or whatever they're called, followed Brother Chisholm one Sunday after doin' some worshipin' and fellowshippin' at First Holy Roller, or whatever that place is called—"

"Holiness Temple. Is that the one?"

"Yeah," said T.J. as he exhaled. "So, as I was sayin', this parishioner followed Brother Chisholm after Sunday services. Seems like he was suspicious. Turns out, Brother Chisholm was off to do a different kind of holy rollin' over to Miss Lula's out on the DeLand Highway."

Ronnie grinned. "I've lost more money at Lula's than I can remember."

"If you wouldn't play craps while stone drunk, then you'd remember," said T.J. with a wink.

Laughing, Ronnie said, "I drink so I'll forget, 'cause I'm lousy at craps."

T.J. sucked in another long drag on his Camel and then exhaled, coughing as he did. "This parishioner was a tourist—"

"They're the worst."

"Don't I know it? Anyways, when Mr. Tourist Parishioner found out the what's what and the who's who at Miss Lula's, he went right over to Chief Johnson—"

"Who was in no way surprised," said Ronnie as he stubbed out his cigarette in the ashtray T.J. kept out for the convenience of his customers.

"Don't you know it? Since Chief Johnson and Miss Lula..." He wiggled his eyebrows at Ronnie as he took one last draw on his cigarette, getting it all the way down to his fingertips, and then crushing it out in the ashtray.

"You think they...?" Ronnie made a vulgar motion with his two hands.

"I don't know nuthin' about the matin' habits of police chiefs in Central Florida, but what I do know is how this was one instance where Chief Johnson couldn't turn a blind eye. He got a warrant and went and searched that trailer in Holly Hill that Brother Chisholm kept and that's where he found a huge stack of developed nudies from who knows where."

Ronnie frowned. "Did Johnson try to pin that on you?"

"He sure as hell did and I told him I wouldn't do business with no snake handlin' hypocrite." He winked at Ronnie. "I prefer my customers to be out-and-out sinners." He pulled out another Camel and lit it without offering one to Ronnie. "I even heard"—he took a long drag on the new cigarette—"that Johnson went over to the beachside and tried to shake down old man Grenell."

Ronnie snorted. "Charles Grenell wouldn't handle nudies any more than the pope would."

"Don't I know it? Back before the war, he was always gettin' on to me for developin' *tasteful art prints for a select crowd of enthusiasts*."

The two men laughed. Ronnie stood up, ready to go. T.J. McClure kept his little shop on the warm side, rarely opening the windows, and, after just a few minutes of being in there, Ronnie was panting for some cool sea breezes.

"So, I can have the prints for you this afternoon," said T.J.

"Good." Ronnie snapped the fingers of his right hand as he remembered the most important part of the job. "And, listen, I need the prints blown up to five by eight. Can you do that?"

"This evidence for Tom Jarrell?" asked T.J. with a slight frown.

"Yeah. And, what you see on the photographs, I need you to keep it all under your hat."

T.J. picked up the cannister and rolled it around in his hand. "Sure thing." He thought for a moment and then looked up at Ronnie. "Say, what they're sayin' about Ben Kirkpatrick's kid? Any truth to that?"

Ronnie grinned and said, "Well, you'll read some about it in those photographs. But it was really Skipper Johnson who took advantage of Howie Kirkpatrick. Skipper had money, a good home, and all the trimmings. All Howie had was a drunk for a father."

T.J. nodded. "I figured it was just more of that bullshit that Gene Mayer likes to peddle. Like him sayin' how Tom Jarrell paid Inez Johnson to leave town." He laughed bitterly. "Like anyone could ever convince that witch to do a damn thing. Not even her husband could control her." He stubbed out his cigarette.

"Wadda ya mean?"

T.J. leaned on his counter again. "I seen Leland and Inez out on the town once. It was back when I was goin' with Sadie. You remember her?"

Ronnie grinned and moved his hands in an hourglass shape. "Sadie, Sadie, lovely lady?"

T.J. chuckled. "She's the one. And, boy, did she know how to go to town below the belt, if you know what I mean. She did that for me one time when we were driving up to Jacksonville. Thank the good Lord it was dark outside." He whistled and then cleared his throat. "Anyways, the two of us was at the Trocadero—"

"The nightclub at the Riviera?"

"That's the one. Anyways, Leland and Inez was there, really puttin' on the dog, and I guess they had too much champagne or somethin' because, next thing you know, she threw a glass of the stuff in his face. He pulled back and walloped her, but good. She didn't cry or nuthin'. She stood up, pulled back herself, and slugged him right on the jaw. A couple of us applauded because it was a real good show."

"Do you know what it was about?"

T.J. reached for his Camels and came up empty. Ronnie pulled out his pack of Lucky Strikes. Once T.J. had one lit and had taken a drag on it, he said, "Sadie was always one for bein' a little nosy and she went to go powder her nose right behind Inez Johnson. After about fifteen minutes, Sadie came back and said she was ready to leave. I paid up and we went out for a walk down to the river before I drove her home." He took another long drag. "Anyways, she tells me how Inez Johnson was in the ladies and just goin' on and on about how her husband didn't know how to raise his own son and she was threatenin' to take Skipper back up to New York City."

"When was that?"

T.J. stood, exhaled, and thought about it. "Huh." He looked at Ronnie. "When'd you move Mrs. Jarrell here?"

"1944."

T.J. nodded and then snapped his fingers. "That's right. It would have been September or October of that year. That was when Sadie left to move down to Miami. In November. " He looked at Ronnie meaningfully. "Remember?"

Ronnie nodded. "Sure." He knew what T.J. was referring to and hoped they could skip over all that and get back to when Inez Johnson slugged her husband in public.

T.J. folded his arms. "It's been a while, Ronnie Grisham."

"You're right about that." Looking at his watch, Ronnie said, "I got to get—"

"I've been dating Rhonda Gillespie for a few months now."

"How's that goin'?" Ronnie tried to look and sound genuinely interested.

T.J. nodded. "Good enough, I suppose. But she's no Sadie." He licked his lips. "And she's no Ronnie Grisham, neither."

Ronnie wanted to get the hell out of that camera shop so bad. He was afraid T.J. would press the subject and want to lock the door and put up the "Back Soon" sign. Ronnie really wished he'd never, ever made it with T.J. McClure. He'd been a fun roll during a dry spell when Ronnie needed some relief, but he was dirty, he stank, and he always wanted to do it in the back in the darkroom. Ronnie hated the smell of all those chemicals, along with all the other nasty bodily aromas.

Plastering a grin on his face, Ronnie said, "I'm late already."

"No dice?" asked T.J., looking a little disappointed.

"Not today."

"I suppose you're giving it all to Tom Jarrell these days. That the case?"

Ronnie sighed. "I'll be back around 5, T.J."

A fierce storm of rage passed over the other man's face. And, as quick as it came, it was gone. With a sigh of resignation, T.J. said, "OK," and disappeared through the curtain and into the back before Ronnie could say anything more.

...

Marveen stared at Tom for a very long moment. She opened her mouth to speak, closed it, then opened it again. "Isn't that illegal?"

Tom was measured in his reply. "The law says nothing on the subject."

Marveen screwed up her face. "Well, you know what I mean..."

Tom was ready for what he wanted to say next. In the back of his mind, he'd been preparing for just that very moment for some time. "How about this? I promise not to ask about what happens when you and Bill

Gordon go out on a date if you promise to do the same." He'd intentionally not mentioned Ronnie's name or his own. He wanted to keep her attention on Bill and away from... other matters.

Marveen blinked a couple of times and opened her mouth again. She closed it and nodded. After a couple of seconds, she said, "That's fair."

Tom took in a deep breath. "I'm glad you asked about this because I've wanted to talk to you about it, but I was waiting for the right time."

She nodded.

"I expect us all to behave professionally at work." He felt like that was the best way to begin. He was also hoping that would be where they would end.

Marveen considered his words for a moment. Then: "So, when you and Ronnie have been in your office, whispering, it's always been about work?"

Tom nodded, feeling relieved. "Yes, that's right. Like I said, I expect us all to behave professionally at work."

She nodded and then looked off to the side. "When Ronnie went down to West Palm Beach and Fort Lauderdale week before last, were the two of you having a fight?"

Tom tried to keep his expression neutral. On the one hand, he was impressed that she could read the two of them so well. And he felt as if he owed it to her to confirm her suspicions. On the other hand, wouldn't that be crossing the line he'd just laid down? He took another deep breath. "Well, we did have a disagreement that day, but Ronnie really did have a job to do down there."

Marveen nodded. Coolly, she said, "So, you're not gonna tell me?" As soon as she said that, her face turned red. Tom could tell she knew she'd just crossed that very same line.

He didn't want her to feel bad, so he smiled and said, "Like I said, I expect us all to behave professionally at work."

Marveen nodded but didn't say anything in reply.

. . .

"Mr. Grisham!"

Ronnie froze. He was in the middle of taking a sponge bath in the room he rented on the second floor of Mabel Baum's boarding house. He was only wearing his shorts. "Yes, Miz Mabel?"

From the other side of the door, she said, "I want to have a word with you, young man."

"I'm a little occupied at the moment."

"Fine," she said. "I'll be waiting for you downstairs."

"Yes, ma'am."

Twenty minutes later, once Ronnie was clothed and combed and feeling refreshed after his encounter with T.J. (during which nothing happened back in the dark-room, thank God, but which left him feeling dirty and in need of a clean-up), he opened his bedroom door and then bounded down the stairs.

As he walked into the front living room, he found Mabel Baum, the owner of the boarding house where he'd been rooming since he'd moved Sarah and Missy to Daytona Beach from Tallahassee back in 1944. Miz Mabel was a no-nonsense woman of about 55 who kept her steel gray hair tied up in a bun and was always bustling around, doing something.

Right at that moment, she was washing the little porcelain figurines she collected and had displayed in the front living room. There were shepherds and shep-herdesses, mostly. She also had a few lambs, a cow or two, and a horse with an oversized mane.

Looking up from her cleaning, she gave Ronnie a scowl. "Where have you been the last two nights?"

With a grin, Ronnie said, "On a case."

"I see," said Miz Mabel as she ran a cloth over one of the larger lambs. "Does that case have anything to do anything with Skipper Johnson's murder?"

"You know I can't talk about my work." He reached over and grabbed the cow. He was hoping that, by touching one of her precious figurines, he could distract her.

She huffed. "Put that down this minute, Mr. Grisham." Ronnie meekly complied, hanging his head a little as he did. She shook her finger up at him. "I've told you again and again that I don't like you handling my things. You're more like a bull in a china shop than any boarder I've ever had."

"But I've never broken anything," protested Ronnie.

"Yes, you have."

Ronnie grinned. "Well, that cane chair was a hundred years old and Mr. Robertson told me to sit on it at the table."

She shook her head, her cheeks flush with irritation. "And, that's another thing, do you have any idea where Everett Robertson has gotten to? I haven't seen him in three days." She vigorously wiped down the cow that Ronnie had picked up.

"No, ma'am. I don't keep track of Mr. Robertson."

She snorted. "And now you call yourself a private detective?" She replaced the cow and bustled away from the bamboo shelves on the left side of the big fireplace and began to attack the figurines scattered among various books stacked in the oak cabinet on the right side.

"I hope you'll excuse me, Miz Mabel, but I need to get back to work."

"Work?" she said with a frown. "Are you planning on moving out?"

Ronnie grinned as hard as he could. "No, ma'am. Why do you ask?"

She held a shepherdess in her hand and looked up at him. "I was reading my cards last night and it said a big change was coming. If you're part of that big change, I hope you'll tell me sooner rather than later."

He nodded. "I promise I will, but I don't know about any big change." He knew he was lying when he said that, but he didn't know what else to do right at that moment other than make his escape out the front door as fast as good manners would let him do so.

...

Tom was back at his desk, considering the case of the duplicate letters from Allied Southern Insurance. He wondered what was really going on in Nashville and why the insurance company thought they could get away with those sorts of denials. It was easy enough to prove that the payments had, in fact, been made on time. All Tom had to do was to ask his clients to go through their cancelled checks from the bank and that would prove their case.

"Marveen?"

Tom couldn't see Marveen at her desk from where he sat. He heard her fumble with something before she answered, "Yes, Mr. Jarrell?"

"Could you come in here? I want to dictate a letter."

"Be right there," came the reply. He thought her voice sounded shaky.

After a moment, she walked into his office, steno pad and pencil in hand, and had a seat in the chair across from his desk. She flipped over the cover on her pad, crossed her legs, and using her knee as a place to hold the pad, looked up expectantly.

Tom was astonished to see her red eyes. It was obvious she had been crying and it hit him hard, although he didn't understand why. He asked, "Are you OK, Marveen?"

She nodded and gave him a weak smile. "I'm sorry, Mr. Jarrell. I was thinking about my uncle."

"Oh?"

"Yes."

As he watched, a tear rolled down her cheek. Reaching into his pocket, Tom pulled out his handkerchief, stood, and walked around his desk to hand it to her.

While she dabbed her eyes with it, he pulled up the second chair he kept for clients and sat down. "What about your uncle?"

She sniffed and held onto the handkerchief. "I always thought he had a heart attack back in '44. But, last night, when Mother and I were talking about..." She dabbed her eyes again. "About you and Ronnie, she told me what really happened."

Tom nodded sympathetically and waited.

"You see, Uncle Jerry is my mother's older brother. Or, he was. And he lived in Fort Lauderdale from 1932 until the war. In the spring of '42, he got a job in a factory in Tacoma."

"In Washington State?" asked Tom.

"Yes," she sniffed. "I don't know what he did, but it was important work and he was happy to be asked to move there, even though, as Mother said, he really was a natural-born beach bum."

Tom smiled at that.

"Well, anyway, in June of '44, Mother got a telegram that he had passed away. Things being what they were, she wasn't able to go up there and, for whatever reason, the county wouldn't ship, um, the body back to Florida, so they cremated him. Daddy..." She looked at

Tom searchingly. "I'm sure you knew, but Daddy was a sergeant for the Daytona P.D."

"Yes, you told me when I interviewed you."

She nodded. "And, you know he died in the summer of '41, right?"

"Yes."

"So, Mother called Sergeant Ashbie—"

"Henry Ashbie?"

"Yes. He and Daddy were real good friends. Do you know him?"

"In passing," said Tom.

"Well, Mother asked Sergeant Ashbie to see what he could find out from up in Washington State about Uncle Jerry and he did." Another tear rolled down her cheek.

Tom patted her arm. "You don't have to tell me about this, if you don't want."

She nodded. "I know, but I do..." She sniffed.

Tom sat back a little and waited.

"Mother told me last night that what Sergeant Ashbie found out about Uncle Jerry was that he didn't die from a heart attack." She frowned a little. "Well, I think he did. But there was another reason, too."

"Underlying causes?"

"No, it was a different word."

"Contributing?"

She nodded. "That's the one. The contributing cause to his heart attack was from being attacked by a man." She wiped her cheek again. "And, you see, Mr. Jarrell, what has me upset is I can't help but think something like that could happen to you or Ronnie."

Tom leaned forward. "Was he attacked by the other man because he made a pass?"

Nodding wordlessly, Marveen sniffed again.

"Well, I wouldn't worry too much about Ronnie because there's nobody in town who ever walks away from a fight with him. He can hold his own, and more."

She smiled a little at that.

"And, as for me, I only have eyes for one person, so there's not much chance something like that would happen to me."

Shyly, she asked, "You mean you only have eyes for Ronnie?"

Tom nodded.

Looking down at the floor, Marveen didn't say anything. Finally, she looked up. "May I ask you a personal question, Mr. Jarrell?"

Tom felt himself stiffen. But the poor girl had just poured out her heart about how worried she was about Ronnie and him, so how could he refuse her without being even more of a heel than he'd already been? So, he smiled a little and said, "Sure."

"Have you ever been on a date with Ronnie?"

Tom sat back and laughed in spite of his immediate embarrassment, which he tried to cover. "Well, not in the way you have. He's never taken me to the movies. But that's not something we would do."

She tilted her head a little. "Why not?"

Tom blinked and tried to come up with a reasonable and honest answer. After a moment, he said, "Well, I'm not saying I wouldn't like that. I would. But Daytona is a small enough town that people would probably wonder what two grown men, particularly two tall grown men, were doing sitting next to each other at the Empire or the Florida."

She giggled. "I guess you're right about that." After a moment, she asked, "But you could go out to dinner—at the New Yorker, for example. If anyone asked, you could say it was a business meeting."

Tom nodded. "Well, Saturday before last, I did take Howie out to the New Yorker for a steak dinner."

Marveen looked shocked for a moment and then opened her mouth, like she did when she was about to say something. She blinked twice and then twice again. "Howie and Skipper? They were in love?"

Tom nodded. "Yes, but that's client confidential information, Marveen."

She nodded. "Of course." She opened her mouth again and then closed it. "That was when I started wondering what was going on here."

"When was that?"

"When you were first interviewing Howie, you kept asking him about the girls Skipper was dating and there was something about that I just plain didn't understand."

Tom nodded slowly. "Yes, I was trying to figure out the nature of Howie's relationship to Skipper."

"And that was how you knew?"

Not wanting to talk about things Howie had said to him in confidence, Tom said, "Well, that was one of the ways."

She took a deep breath and then sighed. "I understand."

Reaching over, Tom patted her arm again. "Thank you for your concern, Marveen."

She nodded.

"And I'm very sorry to hear about your uncle."

"Thank you, Mr. Jarrell." She started to hand back his handkerchief and then pulled it back. "I'll launder this and bring it back to the office tomorrow." She stuffed it in her skirt pocket.

Tom nodded with a smile and then stood, walked around to behind his desk, and sat. "Thank you, Marveen, for your confidence and for your excellent work."

She flipped open her steno pad and said, "And thank you, Mr. Jarrell. I..." She stopped for a moment before continuing, "I think I'm really going to enjoy working for you for as long as you'll have me."

He smiled. "I'm very glad to hear that. Now, I need you to send the same letter to three clients."

Her pencil poised, Marveen leaned forward and then began to make shorthand notes as Tom dictated the text of the letter to her.

Chapter 7

761 S. Palmetto Avenue
Friday, September 26, 1947
A few minutes past 7 in the morning

Alice enjoyed walking to work along Palmetto in the mornings. She could have taken the first bus, but, unless it was raining, preferred to walk.

Her house, which she shared with her Aunt Mary, was at the corner of Washington and Madison. That morning, it had still been dark outside with just a hint of purple in the sky, when she'd started her daily walk across town.

She would usually zig-zag her way over to Second Avenue and Ridgewood and then cross down to the very start of Palmetto. From there, she followed it through downtown and into the leafy neighborhood of homes from the turn of the century and then into the section where Mr. Jarrell lived, just shy of the corner of Bellevue.

As she walked, her thoughts drifted towards the plans she had for the weekend. Betsy, her gal, who lived in DeLand, was driving over on Saturday morning. They were planning on taking a drive down towards the colored beach south of New Smyrna and spending the afternoon there, enjoying a picnic lunch, before driving back to Daytona.

She hadn't talked it over with her Aunt Mary, but Alice wanted to ask Betsy to stay the night at the house on Washington. It was a daring thing to do. Alice knew her Aunt Mary had a general kind of notion about the nature of their relations, but Alice had been careful not to be too forward about it all.

Crossing South Street, she looked at her watch as she finished the last block of her two-and-a-half-mile morning trek. It was 20 past 7, which was perfect timing, once again. Smiling at herself for being a bit early one more day, she wondered if Mr. Ronnie Grisham would be joining her and Mr. Tom for breakfast that morning. If so, that would make three nights in a row for the two men to share the same bed, something she very much approved of.

After reaching over to pick up the *Morning Journal*, left on the front yard, Alice made her way around the back of the house and stopped short.

Sitting on the back porch were two white girls. One was blonde, with curly hair, and the other was a brunette. They were leaning against each other, whispering under the Spanish moss that hung down from the massive live oak whose limbs stretched across most of Mr. Tom's backyard. Alice immediately saw their kind of intimacy for what it was. Even as young as they might be (Alice never could quite tell the age of most white folks), she knew they were lovers. It was unmistakable.

Clearing her throat, Alice boldly walked over to the porch, startling the young girls as she did.

The blonde, who looked a lot like Shirley Temple, glanced up. "Oh! I'm sorry."

Alice wanted to smile but had to make sure who the girls were (although she was certain she knew) and not act too friendly. "May I help you?"

The brunette was scared and leaned into her friend. The blonde asked, "Is this Mr. Jarrell's house?"

"Yes, ma'am, it is. It's awfully early to come calling, though."

The blonde nodded apologetically. "I know. My friend, Bobby Caldwell, drove us down here early this morning."

"Drove you down from where?" asked Alice, more and more certain she knew who the girls were.

"From Saint Augustine," replied the blonde, a little less apologetically and a little more sure of herself. Alice liked that. A young girl in love needed to be sure of herself.

Looking around the porch for evidence of luggage, Alice saw two suitcases underneath the kitchen window. "I suppose you're here to see Mr. Tom about Skipper Johnson?"

The brunette gasped while the blonde held up her head and nodded. "We are. Will you let him know we're here?"

Alice finally grinned. "I sure will. Why don't you two get up and let me through? I'll get coffee on and then we'll go from there." The two girls stood up and made room for Alice to walk up the back steps. As she walked by the two of them, she said, "It's nice to meet you, Miss Pauline Thompson."

It was the blonde's turn to gasp. "How'd you know my name?"

"Oh, honey," said Alice as she opened the back door. "I've been wonderin' when the two of you would show up. I knew it was just a matter of time."

. . .

Tom thought he heard voices in the backyard, outside the bedroom window, but then decided he was probably dreaming. He opened his eyes and looked at Ronnie's chest, rising and falling as he slept. It was their third night in a row and Tom was beginning to believe that he didn't want Ronnie to ever go back to Mabel Baum's boarding house over on Third Avenue.

He leaned over, kissed Ronnie's stubble-covered face, and whispered, "Good morning."

With a snort, his lover opened his eyes and then turned over on his side with a smile. "Mornin'."

Tom was about to kiss him again when he heard a sharp rap on the bedroom door. "Mr. Tom?" It was Alice.

"Yes?"

"You got company."

Tom sat up, pulling the sheet over his chest protectively. "What time is it?"

"Half past 7. It's Pauline Thompson and her girlfriend, all the way down from Saint Augustine."

Ronnie laughed and said, "Well, it's about time."

Alice laughed on the other side of the door. "That's what I just told 'em."

Tom, feeling a little confused, said, "We'll be right out, as soon as we can get dressed."

"Yes, sir. And good morning to you both."

"Mornin'!" replied Ronnie as he reached his arms around Tom and kissed him on the back of the neck.

. . .

Ronnie pulled on the shirt he'd been wearing the night before and watched Tom do the same thing. He was real glad to be waking up a third morning with the man he loved. He hoped it was just the beginning of a whole lifetime of such mornings, although he didn't want to startle Tom, who could be a little bit like a deer when it came to matters of the heart. Ronnie knew he had to walk slowly, not make any sudden movements, and let Tom come around to the idea on his own, and in his own time. If that meant another night or two over at Miz Mabel's, Ronnie was fine with that.

Getting back to the matter at hand, however, he grinned over at Tom and said, "I figured these two girls would show up. Just not so danged early in the mornin'."

Tom stopped what he was doing and frowned, the crease in his forehead forming as he did. "Why did you and Alice think they would be coming to see me?"

Ronnie walked over and began to button Tom's shirt. "Because I was pretty sure when that affidavit made its way into Gene Mayer's grubby little hands, he would tell his client, Leland Johnson, who would then call up to Saint Augustine to let his good friend, Mr. Roger Thompson, know that the truth about his daughter was gonna be discussed in open court next week." He kissed Tom on the nose. "I hope he didn't beat her."

Tom nodded and kissed Ronnie quickly on the lips. "Me too."

...

Tom led the way down the hall and around the corner into the living room. He was surprised to see the two girls, one blonde and one brunette, sitting at the dining table, both with cups of coffee in their hands. The cups were part of the "good" china Sarah's parents had given them when they married back in 1939. It was white with little blue and purple flowers strung together along green vines. The little silver tray a cousin of Sarah's had given them as a wedding present, complete with matching creamer and sugar bowl, part of that same set of china, sat in front of them.

Tom rarely ate there, usually taking his meals in the kitchen with Alice when she was around. Then he realized Alice was treating the young ladies like the company they, in fact, were.

Tom took a look at the two girls. He normally didn't put too much attention on such things, but, for some reason, found himself detailing the girls' features, as if he was narrating a crime novel.

As he got a good look at the blonde, he realized how much she looked like Shirley Temple, with her blonde curls. She didn't have the same perky nose, however. Hers was straight and a little wider.

The brunette, who had startling blue eyes, was a little chubbier than the blonde, who was definitely curvy. Her pouty lips were cherry red and he was pretty sure that was their natural color and that she wasn't wearing any makeup.

Of the two, Tom immediately found himself drawn to the brunette even though he wasn't even sure who was who.

The blonde looked up from her coffee and smiled. It was what the books called, "a winning smile." Her teeth were perfectly straight and white.

The brunette copied her friend's moves. She smiled. Her teeth were smaller and not as white but still nice and straight.

In a flash, Tom could understand why the two girls would be a perfect for each other. It was obvious to him they were two best friends who were in love with each other. Tom felt a pang of regret as he remembered that summer after high school when he thought he and Ronnie would be together forever.

Remembering himself, Tom smiled and said, "Good morning, ladies. I'm Tom Jarrell and this is my friend, Ronnie Grisham."

The blonde's smile widened. "Good morning, Mr. Jarrell and Mr. Grisham. I'm Pauline Thompson and"—she looked at the other girl fondly—"this is Elizabeth Newkirk, *my friend*." She said the last two words in such a way that left no doubt in Tom's mind that he was right about the nature of their relationship.

Right then, Alice walked in with two cups of coffee, with matching saucers, both from the "good" china. She handed one to Tom and then the other to Ronnie. With a friendly smile, she said, "Breakfast will be ready in about fifteen minutes." Alice then disappeared back into the kitchen.

...

Ronnie loved watching Tom do his job. Right then, at the dinner table, he was gently questioning the two young gals from Saint Augustine. Ronnie was sipping on his coffee (he was glad to see Sarah's good china being used and out for once—he'd always thought it was real pretty) and watching Tom and how he could ask a question, open-ended like, and just let the answers come tumbling out. It made Ronnie all excited, truth be told, but he managed to control himself, particularly when handling Sarah's good china.

"So," said Tom, "your father got a call last night?"

The blonde, Pauline, nodded. "Yes, sir. It was from Mr. Johnson. I knew because I was the one who answered the phone when it rang. And Mr. Johnson,"—she looked at the brunette, Elizabeth, but everyone called her Bessie—"he's always so nasty on the telephone. I never liked him."

Bessie nodded. "He's just not very nice. My father did business with him and I always thought he was a real creep."

Ronnie watched Tom's face closely to see if he smiled at that. To his credit, he didn't. He just kept going with his questions. "Do you know what Mr. Johnson said to your father?" That was directed at Pauline.

She nodded. "He told Dad that Mrs. Johnson, Skipper's mother, had filed some sort of paper saying how I was..." She looked over at Bessie, who hung her head a little.

Ronnie, unable to help himself, said, "That you were an invert, like Mr. Jarrell and me." He then added, "And Alice."

Bessie jerked her head up. "Colored can be like us too?"

Ronnie thought he heard Alice cough in the kitchen, but he wasn't sure.

Tom nodded. "Anyone can be an invert, Bessie." He looked at Pauline. "What happened after your father got the call from Mr. Johnson?"

She sighed. "Well, he yelled at me for a good long while, not that I paid much attention. I was working for a friend of his in Saint Augustine, a lawyer by the name of Leroy Robbins. He told me he was going to call Mr. Robbins this morning and tell him I quit and then he was going to take me to Chattahoochee and have me committed."

Ronnie shook his head. "That loony bin place is awful. Why, I knew—" He was relieved when Tom interrupted him before he could stupidly tell the poor gals something that would likely scare them even more than they were already.

"So, what did you do after that?" Tom's voice was soft and soothing.

"Well," replied Pauline, "I came up with a plan, something I've been thinking about for a while. I apologized to my father, in a general sort of way, and told him I would go straight to bed and be ready to leave the next morning." She smiled at Bessie. "He even went up into the attic and got down my suitcase for me, so I could pack it."

Ronnie couldn't help himself. He crossed his arms. "Your pop sounds like a real prince."

Tom frowned at him, but Pauline laughed bitterly. "Oh, Mr. Grisham, you don't know the half of it."

Clearing his throat, Tom went back to his slow and sure interrogation. "What did you do next?"

Pauline sat up straight. "Well—"

Alice walked into the room with a tray of plates and said, "I'm sorry to intrude, but breakfast is ready."

. . .

Once Alice had passed out plates and refilled everyone's coffee, she looked over from the edge of the kitchen door and asked, "Anything else, Mr. Tom?"

He smiled at her. "No, thanks, Alice." He saw Ronnie point at his watch and then tap on it. Leaning over a bit to look at it on Ronnie's thick wrist, Tom realized it was half past 8 already. They would be late getting into the office. He thought about that for a moment and then glanced over at Alice and said, "Thanks."

She smiled, nodded, and disappeared into the kitchen.

Tom stood and said, "Excuse me, ladies. I'll just be a moment."

Pauline's mouth was full, but Bessie replied, "Of course, Mr. Jarrell."

Tom walked over to the spot between the dining room and the kitchen where the phone sat. He picked it up and waited for the operator. After a moment, a voice said, "Number, please."

"517."

"One moment."

He turned to look at Ronnie, who winked at him as he bit into a piece of buttered toast. Tom smiled back. Right then, he heard a female voice say, "Hello?"

"May I speak to Marveen, please?"

"Mr. Jarrell?"

"Yes."

"This is Eugenia Dodge, Marveen's mother."

"Good morning, Mrs. Dodge."

"Good morning to you." She paused for a moment. "Marveen told me all about your conversation with her yesterday."

Tom felt himself blushing. "Oh, she did?"

"Yes, she did. Now, I don't approve but that doesn't mean one thing or another. What I do like is when a man knows himself and—"

Before she could finish, Tom heard some sort of commotion on the other end of the line. After a few seconds of a kind of rustling sound, Marveen spoke. "Mr. Jarrell?"

"Good morning, Marveen."

"Good morning. I am so sorry for my mother's rude behavior." She sounded irritated.

Tom chuckled. "Don't think anything of it. I called to ask if you could come over here instead of going into the office."

"Of course. Is everything OK?"

"Yes. I need you to help me out with something and, well, it's easier if you come over here."

"Of course." She sounded doubtful.

"Oh, and, Marveen?"

"Yes, Mr. Jarrell?"

"Remember that client information is confidential. Even with your mother."

"Oh, of course, Mr. Jarrell. Yes, of course. I completely understand."

Chuckling again, Tom said, "Thank you. See you soon."

"Yes. Goodbye." As she hung up the phone, Tom could hear her say, "Mother!"

Putting the phone on the receiver, Tom walked back over to the dining table and sat down. "Sorry about that. I want my secretary, Marveen Dodge, to come over."

Pauline looked at Bessie and then at Tom. "Why?"

"Because I want you two young ladies to check into a hotel on the beachside for the next few days."

Bessie gasped and Pauline shook her head, saying, "But, Mr. Jarrell, all we have is five dollars between us."

"Don't worry about that. You have to stay somewhere, and I don't think you'd like staying here. Ronnie takes way too long in the bathroom."

The two girls giggled as Ronnie looked at him sideways for a long moment. Tom felt himself blush again. He realized he'd pretty much just asked the man to move in. Clearing his throat and squirming in his chair a little, Tom said, "Let's get back to your story, Pauline. The last thing you said was that your father brought your suitcase down from the attic."

Pauline nodded. "Yes, sir. I immediately started packing, making some noise as I did. I then got into bed with everything but my shoes on, turned off the light, and waited."

"Waited for what?"

"For my dad to go to sleep. He snores awful and I can hear it through the walls."

"I see. Go on," said Tom as he spooned some of Alice's homemade peach jam on a triangle of toast.

"Well, once he was asleep, I grabbed my suitcase and quietly left the house. I then ran over to Bessie's. I hid my suitcase behind the big azalea bush she grows on the northeast corner and—"

Ronnie asked, "What about your mother?"

"She's in Atlanta."

Remembering what Leland Johnson had testified about during Howie's trial, Tom asked, "Was there any truth to there being a house for you and Skipper to move into up in Atlanta?"

Pauline's eyes widened. "What?"

"During Howie's trial, Mr. Johnson said he'd arranged for you and Skipper to be married, had bought a house for you in Atlanta, and was setting up Skipper in a job at a bank up there."

Pauline nodded. "Well, I knew about the first and third part, but I never heard about a house."

"Do you think that's why your mother is up there?"

Before she could say anything, Bessie said, "Tell him why she's in Atlanta, Paul."

Tom and Ronnie quickly exchanged amused glances at the girl's use of a masculine nickname.

Pauline sighed. "She's been in Atlanta for several months. My parents are separated and have been since May. My grandparents live in Atlanta, in a big house on Ponce de Leon, and my mother has been staying with them."

"And you didn't go up with her?" asked Ronnie.

"No, sir. I had my job in Saint Augustine, after all."

Tom asked, "After you got to Bessie's house, what did you do?"

"Well, like I said, I hid my suitcase behind the azalea bush. Then I climbed up the backyard trellis to the second floor and knocked on Bessie's window." She smiled at her girlfriend. "I've been doing that since we were in elementary school."

"What did you do, Bessie?"

"Well, I let Paul in and she quickly told me what happened. So, I got dressed and then got out my suitcase from the closet and packed it. Once that was done, Paul went out the way she came, and I left the house through the front door."

"What about your parents?"

"They were in Jacksonville for the night. My father had a meeting to attend and they decided to stay the night." She added, "I left them a note."

Tom thought the girl sounded a little defensive. He asked, "What'd it say?" and ate some of his scrambled eggs, which were cold.

"That I was leaving with Paul... Well, I said, 'Pauline,' of course."

"Of course," prompted Tom.

"And that I wasn't going to Chattahoochee either."

"Had they threatened to take you there?"

Bessie nodded, looking vacant and upset, but not crying.

"Then what happened?" asked Tom.

Pauline picked up the story. "Then we went over to Bobby Caldwell's apartment. He rents an apartment near Old Town. He's a gay guy, like the two of you, and went to school with us—"

"Although he graduated in 1944," said Bessie.

Pauline nodded. "He was a year ahead of us, but I've known Bobby for as long as I can remember."

Tom nodded. There was something Pauline had said that he didn't understand. He asked, "You said he was a 'gay guy' like us. What do you mean?"

Ronnie snorted as Bessie and Pauline giggled. Tom

wasn't sure, but he thought he heard Alice laugh in the kitchen. Looking over at Ronnie, he said, "What?"

Leaning over and kissing Tom on the nose, Ronnie said, "It's another word for invert."

"Oh," said Tom, looking at Pauline. "I've never heard it used like that."

She smiled. "I read about it in one of those books you can order that comes wrapped in brown paper."

Bessie giggled. "Paul showed me one of hers when we were in high school. It was called, *The Brave Ones*, and was all about some kids in New York City."

Ronnie laughed. "I think I read that one."

Tom shook his head, feeling hopelessly old-fashioned. Before he could ask his next question, he heard someone knocking on the front door.

...

Marveen pulled up into Mr. Jarrell's driveway and parked her old DeSoto behind his Buick. She was still fuming about her mother. How dare she say things like that to her boss?

She stepped out of the car, pulling her purse with her, and then closed the door. Although she knew where Mr. Jarrell lived, she'd never been to his house before.

It was a nice place, but rather small. Her mother said it was built in the early 20s before the real estate bust. The lawn was well-kept, which was nice too. She heard the sound of children playing across the street. Turning, she realized the house was directly behind the grade school on Ridgewood. It occurred to her that, were she still alive, Missy Jarrell would have been one of those children. She wasn't sure, but she thought Missy would have been in the second grade that year.

With a sigh, she turned back towards the house and

tried to put that melancholic thought out of her mind as she walked across the grass and up the couple of steps to the front door.

She knocked and waited.

After a few moments, the door opened and she saw Mr. Jarrell standing just inside, wearing the same shirt he'd worn the day before. He gave her his usual small smile and said, "Come in, Marveen."

She did that and looked around. The door opened right into the living room which was comfortably furnished. Only about a third of a wall separated the dining room from the living. At the nice mahogany-colored table sat two girls of about 20 or so. And, of course, Ronnie Grisham was standing there, grinning like he always did, and wearing the same clothes he'd worn the day before. He'd obviously spent the night, hopefully in the guest bedroom, but she doubted that would be the case. Marveen wasn't sure how she felt about that, not that it was any of her business.

As Mr. Jarrell introduced the two girls, Marveen suddenly realized who the blonde was. She was the one Skipper was supposed to marry. That would mean the brunette was her "friend." Marveen sighed. She supposed it was inevitable that her life would be filled with people like this. And she hoped Mr. Jarrell wasn't expecting her to spend any time with either Pauline or Bessie. That would be just too, too queer for her.

Mr. Jarrell was motioning for her to sit at the dining table, so she did, taking the chair at the end, by the little hall that led to the kitchen.

"Alice?" said Mr. Jarrell as he stepped into the hall.

"Yes, sir?" came the reply. Marveen suddenly remembered that Alice was the colored maid who cooked and cleaned for Mr. Jarrell. And, she supposed, for Ronnie Grisham too. Now.

Putting his hand on her shoulder, Mr. Jarrell asked, "Did you have breakfast already?"

"Yes, sir. Thanks."

"How about some coffee?"

"That would be nice. Thanks."

"Alice? Could you bring a cup of coffee in for Marveen?"

"Yes, sir," came the reply from the kitchen.

As she looked around the room at the people seated at the table, Marveen wondered what Sarah Jarrell would have thought about everyone assembled. She was probably spinning in her grave, thought Marveen to herself as she smiled at the two girls who really looked like they needed a good bath and a brush run through their hair, particularly Pauline. She wondered how they'd gotten down to Daytona Beach from Saint Augustine. Probably hitchhiked, she thought. And that would make sense. They were obviously running away from their families. She suddenly realized the blonde, Pauline, reminded her of a tomboy version of Shirley Temple.

Mr. Jarrell was suddenly introducing her to Alice. The colored maid, who could really stand to lose some weight, politely handed her a cup of coffee. The china pattern was nice. Marveen figured it was probably the good china that someone had given Mr. and Mrs. Jarrell as a wedding gift.

Smiling and nodding, Marveen decided she was just going to have to put on her church face, one she'd practiced on Sundays and Wednesday nights at Second Baptist, and that was the best way to get through how uncomfortable she felt sitting at a dead woman's dining table in such strange and queer company.

. . .

"Now that Marveen is here, and settled, let's continue." Tom glanced over at his secretary who looked uncomfortable for some reason. He supposed she knew who Pauline and Bessie were as well as the nature of their relationship. He sighed, realizing there was nothing he could do right then, and hoping she would grin and bear it, making the best of the situation as well as she could.

Ronnie said, "We were talking about Bobby Caldwell."

Pauline nodded. "So, we went over to his apartment, but he wasn't home yet from his job. He waits tables at the City Gates Restaurant in Old Town."

Bessie added, "So, we waited for him at the bottom of his stairs."

"He got home at about half past midnight," continued Pauline. "We slept in his bed and he slept on the couch."

"But then we were up at 5 and out the door by 5:30 and on our way here, arriving around 7," finished Bessie.

"And where did your friend go after he dropped you off here?"

"Lauderdale," said Pauline. She glanced over at Marveen before adding, "His beau lives down there, so he goes down on his days off when he can."

Tom nodded. He tried to recap the girls' story in his mind to see if there were any gaps that needed to be filled. Not able to see any, he looked at Marveen. "I want to put them up somewhere beachside for a week or so. Do you have any suggestions?"

Ronnie said, "How about the New Cortez on Atlantic?"

Marveen nodded. "That's nice but not ritzy like the Plaza."

Tom smiled. "Good. Will you drive them over there?" He turned to the girls. "Once you get settled in, just call over to the office if you need anything." Tom looked at Marveen who, he thought, was looking panicked. He abruptly stood and, walking towards the kitchen, said, "Marveen? Can I see you for a moment?"

. . .

"I can't, Mr. Jarrell." Marveen was trying as hard as she could not to run out of there and just go back home and find another job. She took a deep breath as they stood at the far end of his yard near a group of sad and straggly tomato plants that weren't doing much of anything.

"I understand it's an odd situation for you, but I do need your help with this. I don't think it would be a good idea for Ronnie or I to be seen driving the two of them around. No one will think twice if you're driving with two girls about your age."

Marveen sucked in her breath. "I know. But couldn't Alice take them over?"

Mr. Jarrell frowned down at her something awful. "What if Alice got stopped by the police on her way back? She could go to jail."

Marveen knew that. "I'm sorry."

"Me too." He sighed and looked over her head. "We're going to be dealing with a lot of unsavory characters as time goes by. Murderers, thieves, unfaithful husbands..."

Without knowing why, Marveen giggled at the last thing Mr. Jarrell said.

He looked down at her and said, "You wouldn't know this, but the parents of those two girls wanted to commit them to Chattahoochee. They're here because I filed Mrs. Johnson's affidavit on Wednesday and

Pauline's father received a call from Leland Thompson telling him what the affidavit said. It's the least we can do to treat them kindly."

He was right. Marveen knew she was being ridiculous. But the whole thing... Mr. Jarrell and Ronnie wearing their clothes from the day before... Meaning they had slept together in the house... And probably in Sarah Jarrell's bed... And those two girls, sitting at Mrs. Jarrell's table, drinking from her good china that her parents had probably given her... It was just too much.

She knew it wasn't right, but she couldn't shake the icky feeling she had when she thought about all of it.

Out of the blue, Mr. Jarrell said, "I would hope that, if your uncle had run into trouble like this, someone up in Tacoma would have been kind enough to help him out."

That finally did it. That brought her back to her senses. Looking up, she said, "You're right, Mr. Jarrell. Those girls are just girls and they're frightened and they need our help."

Patting her on the shoulder, Tom said, "Thank you, Marveen."

Chapter 8

761 S. Palmetto Avenue
Sunday, September 28, 1947
Half past 9 in the morning

Tom was feeling nervous and he couldn't quite understand why. As he made the bed in his bedroom and picked up the various articles of clothing that Ronnie had left scattered around, he thought maybe he wasn't really enjoying sharing the house with his best friend and lover as much as he thought he would.

He tried to imagine what Sarah would say about the arrangement. But, try as he might, he couldn't think of anything comparable that they had ever discussed. He hoped she didn't mind that Ronnie was sleeping on her side of the bed and leaving his socks on the top of the dresser. Tom wasn't fastidious, by any stretch, but the chair in the bedroom, to his mind, was where all of the previous day's clothes were supposed to rest overnight, to be collected the next morning. Until Ronnie had, more or less, moved in, Tom had tried to pick up the bedroom for when Alice came through to clean each weekday. On the weekends, he made his own bed and put things away. But Ronnie didn't seem to have any interest in doing the same.

Tom had never been over to see his room at Mabel Baum's. He assumed that, in such a small space, Ronnie would have kept things tidy. He also assumed that Mabel would have come through once a day or, maybe, once every other day and cleaned the room by changing the sheets on the bed and running the carpet sweeper or sweeping the room with a broom. He had no idea what the place looked like but, having seen Mabel Baum out and about, he felt certain she kept a tidy house and would have yelled at Ronnie for being a slob.

As he smoothed out the light blue chenille bedspread that Sarah had loved so much, he wondered if maybe he needed to sit down and talk to Ronnie about chores and all that entailed. Sighing to himself, he realized that would mean talking about the two of them living together for the long term.

Standing, Tom turned and looked out the window. The Spanish moss was swaying gently, and he realized that what had him so nervous was the fact that he wasn't sure about the two of them living together. The long term... That he was sure of. That he loved Ronnie Grisham and had always loved him since he ran into him that first day at Leon High... He was certain of that. He could easily see the two of them sitting in rocking chairs on a front porch somewhere, watching rocket ships take off in the distance for the Moon or wherever they would be headed. He knew that Ronnie was his future.

But, as fun as it might be to go to the Moon for a long weekend, Tom lived in the present. And, in the present, two grown men, particularly two tall grown men, living together in a house which one of them had previously shared with a recently-deceased spouse—

Tom stopped and sat down on the bed. Sarah wasn't a "spouse." She was a real person. Someone he'd been in love with, in his own way. The more he thought about what Ronnie had told him about how Sarah had admitted she knew the two men were in love with each other, the more he believed him.

Sarah really had no faults that he could remember. She had been unfailingly kind. She had loved Missy like he'd never seen any parent love their child. He never once saw her strike the girl. He certainly hadn't. A man of his height had no business hitting anyone, much less a small girl. It was unfair. Not that it stopped Ronnie any, but he was different. But even Ronnie would never have even swatted Missy on the behind. Of that, Tom was certain.

He sat on the bed and looked out at the grass in the backyard. He could see Missy playing with a jump rope or tossing a ball in the air. He remembered the day Ronnie had decided to teach her how to play baseball and had begun to show her the ins and outs of throwing a ball. He remembered looking at Sarah as the two of them watched Ronnie and Missy playing. She'd turned to Tom and said, "He's like a big, overgrown kid, isn't he?" Tom had nodded and felt that terrible conflicted feeling that was a hallmark of his days during law school in DeLand before the war and for the year and a half since he'd been back from Germany. He liked Sarah. He loved her, in his own way. But he also loved Ronnie. He truly and deeply loved Ronnie.

That conflict had been unbearable at times. He'd spent days at work at Mayer & Thornton, before Mr. Mayer had fired him, thinking of ways to tell Ronnie to leave town, to leave him alone, to not come around anymore, to forget any sort of sweet interludes when Sarah and Missy were over in Tampa visiting her relatives.

And, every single time he'd finally decided he would do just that... That he would tell Ronnie it was over... He would see his friend's face, his powerful hands, his long legs, his idiotic grin... And Tom would melt.

"Whatcha doin', bud?"

Tom stood with a start and looked out the window, not turning to acknowledge Ronnie's sudden presence in the room. He pulled his handkerchief out of his pocket and wiped his eyes.

Ronnie walked around the bed and stood next to him in front of the window. He didn't say anything for a long while. Finally: "I miss 'em too, you know."

Tom wiped his eyes again and blew his nose. "I know."

. . .

"I don't wanna press you, Tom, but I gotta tell Miz Mabel somethin'." Ronnie was driving the two of them slowly along the beach. They'd just had a lunch of fried fish down at Ponce Park and were making their way back up to Main Street. The tourists were mostly gone and the few locals who were out and about were few, indeed.

Tom, whose left hand had been resting in Ronnie's lap, stirred but didn't say anything. Ronnie figured he wasn't sure what he wanted which was a typical way for Tom to act when confronted with something important. It was how his pal had ended up married back in '39, not that Ronnie resented that since he'd liked Sarah, hell, he'd loved her as much as Tom had, only without sharing a bed.

After several minutes of silence, Ronnie tried another tack. "How about you and me buy ourselves a house beachside? You could front me my half and I'll pay you back as—"

"No," said Tom with a surprising finality.

"OK." Ronnie was hurt by that. He knew Tom had enough cash to buy any house on the market, including a fancy one Ronnie had seen for sale on Peninsula Drive with a riverfront yard and three gigantic live oaks, dripping with Spanish moss. He figured he was stepping over the line and that was OK, but—

"It's our money. If we buy a house, *we* buy a house."

Ronnie looked over at Tom, truly shocked. "What?"

Keeping his eyes on the ocean to his right, Tom said, "I know who told Sarah to buy all those life insurance policies. It wasn't her idea."

Ronnie laughed. "You're wrong there, bud. It was most certainly her idea. She read a short story in the *Saturday Evening Post* or somewheres like that." After checking the rear-view mirror, Ronnie quickly leaned over and kissed Tom's ear. "I'm proud you think I was that smart, but it was all Sarah. I'll admit she asked if I thought it was a good idea. All I told her was to wait until the war was over. I figured—"

"Stop the car, Ronnie."

Doing just that, right where they were, Ronnie looked over at his pal. "What?"

Tom was bent over, untying his shoes.

"What are you doin' there, bud?"

"I want to go wading in the water."

With something between a snort and a giggle, Ronnie asked, "Did hell just freeze over?"

Tom laughed as he began to roll up his trousers. Once he got them high enough, he unfastened his garters. Thanks to his skinny-ass legs, his socks fell right off when he did that.

"Well?" asked Tom. "Don't you want to go in with me?"

Ronnie began to kick his shoes off and then opened his door. "Sure thing, bud."

. . .

When Tom was a kid—it was the summer of 1927, so he was 10 years old—his parents had decided to spend a couple of weeks at Daytona to get out of the stifling heat of Tallahassee. They'd booked a room at the Plaza Hotel right on the beach. Tom had made friends with some of the other kids who were there with their parents and the group of them set about to explore the hotel and the beach. One day they'd been playing in the surf and Tom had seen a pretty blue and purple thing floating in the water. As he'd walked towards it, something had brushed against his leg and he felt as if a thousand knives were cutting him. It had been a Portuguese man o' war, a kind of jellyfish. He was lucky it hadn't killed him. And the memory of the pain had kept him out of the water ever since then.

But on that Sunday, riding in his own car with Ronnie driving, he'd decided he was ready to get back in. He didn't own a pair of swim trunks. Why would he? But he could kick off his socks and shoes and roll up his trousers and wade in.

As he and Ronnie left the car far enough away from the surf so that it didn't get wet, they walked into the water until it was just past their calves. They'd both rolled up their trousers to just above their knees and, as far as Tom was concerned, he didn't care whether his pants got wet or not.

The water was a little chilly at first, but the sun was warm even if the breeze off the ocean was cool. It was a big, blue sky of a day with some clouds out over the ocean in the distance. It looked like it might be raining ten or twenty miles off the coast, but Tom didn't care if it all blew in and rained right where they stood.

Standing in the water, letting the tide come in and flow out, was exhilarating. Tom wondered why he'd waited 20 years to get back into the water even as he kept one eye out for anything pretty that might be floating in the water.

"You look like you're enjoying this, bud."

Tom turned and looked at Ronnie who had also rolled up his shirt sleeves to well above his elbows. Nodding, Tom said, "I am."

With as big a grin as he'd ever seen on his friend's face, and that was saying a lot, Ronnie said, "Good. I like it when you're happy."

Tom stood there for a moment. "You really do love me, don't you?"

Ronnie frowned slightly with less of a grin and more of a smile. "Of course, ever since—"

"Ever since that day at Leon High."

"Yeah. It was love at first sight."

Tom nodded, realizing he was grinning.

"And you were such a pipsqueak then." Ronnie angled around and looked at Tom's backside. "Too bad you never gained any weight. You just stretched out."

Tom laughed at that, feeling embarrassed and loved at the same time. "Well, you gained all that weight for me."

Ronnie made a pose like the muscle men did, showing off the white of his biceps as he did.

Looking up and down the beach very cautiously and realizing the only other cars he could see were off in the distance, a couple of miles away, if that close, Tom walked up and kissed Ronnie right on the lips for a long, passionate moment.

. . .

"Well, what about it, bud?"

"What about what?" replied Tom.

Ronnie was driving them up the beach. They'd just passed the Silver Beach entrance and there were more cars and people than there had been down near Ponce Park earlier when Tom had kicked off his shoes, waded out into the water, and kissed Ronnie right there. As he watched out for kids running across the beach, Ronnie felt himself flush again at the memory.

"What about what?" repeated Tom.

"About buying a house beachside."

Tom sighed and patted Ronnie's leg. "I don't know."

"It ain't the dough, is it?"

"Of course not. We're set."

Ronnie felt that warm feeling again when Tom said that. It was a new sensation and had surprised him when it happened earlier. He'd never even thought of him and Tom being hitched together like that, sharing their money. It was a whole new way of looking at things and Ronnie liked it.

He wasn't greedy, but, all his life, he'd scraped by, always worried about the next month's rent, or week's, depending on where he was living. If they were really in it together, he knew he didn't have anything to be worried about. It felt like a huge weight was suddenly gone. And he liked that feeling.

"It's the fact of us living together," said Tom.

Ronnie nodded. He'd thought about the same thing, himself. He'd already chided himself for not cleaning up after himself that morning. He'd caught Tom picking up his clothes in the bedroom and realized he would have to be more thoughtful in the future and make more of an effort.

"I want to live with you, Ronnie, I do. It's what other people will think that's worrying me."

So, it wasn't the fact that he could be a slob if he wasn't careful. It was other people. Well, that was bullshit and he knew it. "What could happen?"

Tom jerked his head over and stared at Ronnie. "What do you mean?"

Ronnie glanced over quickly. "What's the worse that could happen?"

"What do you mean?" repeated Tom.

"What's... the... worse...?"

"People would talk about us. I could lose business. We could get arrested. We could go to jail."

Ronnie nodded and laughed. "Sure. All that could happen. But you're a smart lawyer. You're the smartest man I know."

"I don't know about that, but I'm smart enough to know this isn't something to laugh at."

"Why?" asked Ronnie.

"Are you kidding me?"

He put his hand on Tom's skinny leg and said, "No, I'm not. I'm the biggest guy in town, and I know because I've had the fights to prove it. Nobody will mess with me and nobody will mess with you, bud."

Tom shook his head. "This isn't about fighting, Ronnie. This is about the law. We're breaking the law every time we... You know..."

Ronnie laughed in spite of the seriousness of the subject. "We could always leave and go somewhere else. Like Miami."

"Or New York or San Francisco. I know."

"Never New York or San Francisco, bud. Those places are way too cold. I'm for the beach and always will be. Tuscaloosa was way too cold for me. I never felt like I could live forever in any place until I came here." He pointed out at the ocean. "We got the beach and the sun. What more could you want?"

Tom didn't seem to have an answer to that. Right then, they came to the Main Street approach, so Ronnie stuck his arm out the open car window and made a left up onto the pavement.

...

They decided to have supper at the Spaghetti House on Magnolia. Tom looked at his watch. It was just past 7 and the place was about half full. They were both drinking red wine and had both ordered spaghetti and meat balls. Tom was having the minestrone while Ronnie ate a green salad, dressed in something oily from what Tom could see. He looked at Ronnie. "You like that?"

"Sure. Got plenty of garlic." He grinned, of course. "My favorite."

Tom took a sip of his soup and thought one more time about their living situation. He really didn't want to move. He liked the neighborhood, although he didn't know any of his neighbors. Sarah had always said she preferred to live more inland than not, since salt-water rust and corrosion was a very real concern on the beachside. Tom tended to agree with that even though he was good about taking in the Buick to have the thing lubed up regularly. And he always made sure to spray the car down with the garden hose after a trip to the beach. He'd done that very thing earlier, while Ronnie had gone inside to take a nap.

Following his nap, he'd pulled Tom into the bedroom for what Ronnie had jokingly called, "afternoon delight," and Tom couldn't disagree with the phrase. While they'd been fooling around, Tom had begun to have an idea. He took another slurp of his soup and decided it was a good one.

"Whatcha thinkin' about, bud?"

Tom put down his soup spoon. "I don't want to move."

Ronnie nodded, but didn't say anything.

"And I can't imagine you sleeping anywhere other than next to me."

Ronnie started to grin but still didn't say anything.

"So, will you go tell Mabel Baum tomorrow that you're moving in with me..."

"Why?"

"Why what?"

"Why tell her?"

"Because she's a gossip and if you don't tell her the truth, she'll make something up."

"What's the truth, then?"

"Tell her that I'm having trouble being alone in the house since Sarah died and that you're moving in to the guest room as a favor to me. All of that is true."

"The guest room?" asked Ronnie with a frown.

"Yes. You're a slob, Ronnie Grisham. You move your clothes in there, so I don't have to pick up after you. But we sleep in the same bed."

Ronnie, grinless for once, sat back in his chair and pulled out his pack of Lucky Strikes. "That so?"

Tom nodded. "That's so."

Ronnie offered a cigarette which Tom declined. Right then, Marco, the waiter, arrived with two big plates of spaghetti, so Ronnie put his pack back in his pocket and winked at Tom while Marco asked whether they would like any cheese.

Chapter 9

Volusia County Courthouse
120 West Indiana Avenue
DeLand, Fla.
Monday, September 29, 1947
Just past 2 in the afternoon

Judge Frederick looked around the packed courtroom. He then turned to the front. "In the matter of State of Florida versus Leland Johnson, are the parties present?" Tom was sitting two rows back, directly behind the defense table on the left. Ronnie was up in the colored gallery, above the jury box. It had the best view in the courtroom.

Tom had his briefcase with him, which included Marveen's shorthand notes and the developed photographs that Ronnie had taken. The blown-up photographs were surprisingly clear and legible.

Mervyn Anderson rose on the right. "The state is present, Your Honor."

Eugene Mayer rose on the left. "The defendant is present, Your Honor."

"Motions?" asked Judge Frederick.

Both lawyers shook their heads in concert.

The judge looked at Anderson. "Opening statement?"

As Mayer sat, Anderson nodded. "Thank you, Your Honor." He turned to the jury, seated against the right wall in a wooden box of two rows of six chairs each with the back row six inches higher than the front, and said, "Ladies and gentlemen of the jury, today you are here because of the intentional death of Roland 'Skipper' Johnson, son of the accused." Anderson then approached the podium. He looked over at Johnson who, from Tom's perspective, a couple of rows back, appeared to be staring straight ahead. "The defendant, an otherwise upstanding citizen of Daytona Beach, founder of Fidelity Trust, a fine banking institution which carried many a business owner during the darkest days of the Depression, capable sailor, a father, and a husband, stands on trial today for the murder, deliberate and intentional, of his only son, Skipper."

Anderson, having kept his focus on Johnson, paused and slowly turned to the jury. "The state intends to prove this and will do so through the introduction of evidence that is plain and simple." He began to count using the thumb of his left hand. "You will hear from a leading physician about how Skipper was struck on the head by an oar out in the middle of the Atlantic Ocean. You will hear from a conscientious police lieutenant about how Skipper's body was found hours later on the sand north of Ormond Beach, having been washed ashore after being pushed into the great Atlantic by its parent. You will have read for you an affidavit from the mother of the deceased, defendant Johnson's own wife, describing, in detail, how the accused went about framing an innocent young man for this very murder and using this very court. You will hear the very testimony of the defendant himself here, in open court only six days ago, that will impeach him, without a single doubt in any of your minds. From these four witnesses: the leading physician, the conscientious police lieutenant, the defendant's wife, and the defendant himself..." Anderson raised his right hand in the air and pointed to the ceiling. His voice suddenly boomed. "You will, no doubt,"—he quickly turned to face Johnson and pointed at him—"find him guilty."

The courtroom was quiet as Anderson returned to his seat. Tom looked over at the jury and saw that several of them were nodding already.

With that, Mr. Mayer leaned forward in his chair. Tom couldn't see him exactly, but he thought the older man was leaning on his folded arms, as if he were trying to sell a used car.

"Well, ladies and gentlemen, I guess you could say that ole Jeremiah has returned and he has found himself a new prophet, one Mervyn Anderson, attorney for the state." Mayer sounded like he was from Arkansas or Kentucky. Tom looked around the room at the other lawyers who had taken the day off to watch the spectacle. They were all smiling. He saw Mr. Thornton, Mr. Mayer's law partner, lean forward and whisper something to Bill Saunders who was grinning and nodding. Looking up at the colored gallery, Tom saw Ronnie was focused on Mayer's face. He noticed the church ladies were not pleased. It wasn't particularly hot, but they all had fans and were whispering disapprovingly among themselves. There were no colored folks on the jury, but Tom figured Mr. Mayer might have crossed a line. He wondered if the white men and women would feel the same way. Based on their grinning expressions, he didn't think so.

Mr. Mayer shrugged and uncrossed his arms, grabbing the arms of his chair and nodding. "I mean, I know I like it when someone tells it like it is. I imagine you do too." He took in a deep breath and made a noise that Tom recognized as his sucking through his teeth. "I mean, I know how much I like it when I know someone is telling it to me straight. You know, my brother-in-law... Some of you may know him,"—Tom saw some heads nodding in the jury box—"well, you see, he's one of the best salesmen I ever met in my whole entire life. Why, he could sell ice to an eskimo." That got a good chuckle from the room. Tom looked over and noticed Judge Frederick was grinning as much as anyone. Tom wondered if he was enjoying the performance.

Mr. Mayer continued his little show. "Well, anyway, when I asked for my wife's hand in marriage, I didn't have a pot to piss in and I asked my brother-in-law to go to the family and help me out a little. You know? Tell them all about my good qualities, although I'm sure Mr. Anderson, here, might wanna tell you they are few and far between." Mr. Mayer then hee-hawed. Tom sat back in his chair, surprised. It sounded like a donkey laughing. But all he did was just say "hee" followed by "haw."

There was a stir in the courtroom. Several jury members leaned forward, as if they were worried that Mr. Mayer might be having a stroke. The lawyer leaned back in his chair and waved his left hand in front of his face. "I'm sorry, ladies and gentlemen. When I get tickled, I make that embarrassin' sound. My wife can't stand it, poor thing. But it just comes out when I think of somethin' funny. And I can't help but think it's funny when I think of what Mr. Anderson might think of me." He put his left hand over his face. Everyone seemed to wait. At the count of three, Mr. Mayer suddenly hee-hawed again.

The courtroom burst into laughter. Tom looked up at the judge who wasn't nearly as amused as everyone else appeared to be, although there was a smile on his face. He gently brought down his gavel and said, "Mr. Mayer, that'll be enough."

Nodding, the lawyer stood and walked to the podium. Tom couldn't help but admire the man's brilliant tactic. He'd disarmed the courtroom, particularly the jury, convincing them he was just a simple, country lawyer, or some such nonsense. He'd also completely diverted all attention away from Anderson's effective and direct opening statement, probably the shortest in the history of the Florida courts.

"Now, ladies and gentlemen." He was still using his aw-shucks voice. "I don't mean to be unkind, but I'm afraid the state's attorney just backed up a truck, maybe one he borrowed, and tried to unload"—Mr. Mayer waved his left hand in front of his nose—"a big pile of manure, fresh from the cow pasture, maybe one of those out by Osteen or Oak Hill. He just tried to tell you a couple of things you're gonna soon find out just ain't right or true."

He leaned back and forth on his feet and then grabbed the podium. "We all know Skipper Johnson is dead. I even understand there was a bit about it in the papers as far away as San Francisco." He thumped the podium and began to raise his voice. "Skipper Johnson is dead and t'ain't nothin' or no one who's gonna bring him back, no ma'am, no sir."

Taking out his handkerchief, he wiped his face. "This is a mighty warm late September afternoon, wouldn't you say?" The day was actually a little cooler than it had been in a while. Tom wondered what his old boss and mentor was up to.

"Now, as I was sayin', ladies and gentlemen, I, uh,

well... now..." He took out his handkerchief again and wiped his face. "My, oh my."

Judge Frederick leaned forward with a concerned expression on his face. "Mr. Mayer?"

The lawyer held up his hand. "I'm fine judge, I'm fine." He took a deep breath and stumbled back to his seat. "I just need to sit for a spell."

Judge Frederick looked at the back of the courtroom. "Louis? Check on Mr. Mayer, please."

The bailiff came jogging forward, pushed through the small swinging doors that separated the gallery from the bar, and knelt next to Mr. Mayer. It seemed to Tom that everyone in the courtroom was holding their breath. After a couple of moments, the sound of Mr. Mayer's head hitting the defense table echoed throughout the courtroom.

. . .

"He's faking. I just know it." Ronnie had crossed his arms and stuck out his long legs. He and Tom were sitting on a bench across the rotunda from the door to the courtroom and had been for almost twenty minutes. The whole building was buzzing, so anything they said to each other couldn't possibly be overheard by anyone else.

Tom sighed and nodded. "Well, he might be. That aw-shucks routine of his was pretty good."

Ronnie laughed in spite of the possibly dire situation. "It sure was. I'm glad I sat up in the colored gallery. I could see his face and he was really on fire." He suddenly remembered something that happened right before Eugene Mayer had stood. "But you know what? His face did turn bright red and then all the blood drained from it."

"When was that?" asked Tom.

"About the time he stood and walked over to the podium."

They sat there for a moment. Tom asked, "Did I tell you Howie's still in Savannah?"

"How many days does that make?"

"Five."

"Well, I hope he's having fun," said Ronnie. "Maybe he's in love."

Before his pal could say anything, Louis Mercer, the bailiff, walked up. "'Scuse me, Mr. Jarrell. Judge wants to see you in chambers."

Ronnie watched as Tom stood and followed the bailiff around the rotunda and into the judge's chambers just off the courtroom. It was a room all the judges shared for when they held court, since most of them had offices in other parts of the county.

Bill Saunders appeared out of nowhere and heavily sat in the spot Tom had been in. "Well, son, what'd you think of all that mess?"

"I think he's faking. What about you?"

Bill crossed his arms over his big belly. "I just heard they loaded Mayer in an ambulance and he's on his way to the district hospital. They say he had a stroke."

"That so?"

"If he's faking, he's doing a damn good job of it."

Ronnie laughed. "What was that hee-haw thing all about it?"

"Just some good ole boy country lawyer lettin' the jury know how *ignerrant* he was, I guess. Seemed to take the steam outta Anderson's openin', that's for sure."

Ronnie nodded and wondered what the judge was saying to Tom right about then.

. . .

"But, Your Honor, I don't believe that would be in Mr. Johnson's best interest," said Tom, feeling exasperated and overwhelmed.

Leaning forward, Judge Frederick said, "No one knows this case better than you and Mr. Anderson and he can't very well be the defendant's attorney."

Tom looked around the room. He was there with Mervyn Anderson, Judge Frederick, Leland Johnson, and L.O. Thornton (Mr. Mayer's law partner). "What about Mr. Thornton?"

The judge nodded. "I'm appointing him your co-counsel, of course. But you know Mayer as well as the rest of us. He never takes anyone into his confidence. No one, other than Mr. Johnson, knows his intention for this trial."

Tom thought as hard as he could. Surely there was someone else who could defend Leland Johnson. Drawing a blank, he asked the next obvious question. "What about a continuance?"

The judge leaned back and looked at Anderson who said, "We're ready this afternoon, Your Honor."

Mr. Thornton, who was looking older and frailer than ever, cleared his throat. "Your Honor, we do require at least a few days before we can proceed. Mr. Jarrell will need to meet with his client—"

Johnson said, "I think ole Tom here will be ready to go by tomorrow. There's not much to tell."

Tom could feel himself panicking but was also curious about what Leland Johnson had just said and why he had such confidence. One thing suddenly occurred to him, so he said it: "But, if I'm not mistaken, Your Honor, Mr. Mayer was planning on bringing me on a hostile witness." He glanced over at Johnson who shifted in his seat.

"Mr. Johnson," said the judge, "you're not required to answer this, but is this the case?"

Johnson seemed to be trying to decide what to say when Anderson spoke up. "I think it's safe for us to stipulate that the state was anticipating this event."

The judge looked at Johnson. "Well?"

Mr. Thornton leaned in and whispered something to Johnson who then nodded and said, "Yes, Your Honor, that was the plan." He cleared his throat. "However, my wife is on her way here."

Everyone in the room turned to Johnson.

"Is that the case?" The judge was staring at Mr. Thornton when he asked that.

Looking genuinely surprised, himself, Mr. Thornton replied, "This is the first I'm hearing of this."

The judge nodded. To Tom, he looked relieved. He then said, "Well, Mr. Jarrell, that lets you off of any conflict of interest since, I assume, Mrs. Johnson was never your client."

Tom said, "That's correct, Your Honor," not at all sure about that. Inez Johnson had paid for Howie's defense, but he didn't want to say that in from of Leland Johnson. He sat back and tried to think of what to say or do next. Everything was happening too fast. Finally, he looked over at Anderson. "What's Mr. Johnson charged with?"

"Manslaughter."

Tom blinked. It was the most obvious case of first-degree murder he could imagine. Leland Johnson had taken his son out on a boat and hit him over the head, intending to kill him, and then dumped his body in the ocean.

In his head, Tom went over all the evidence he knew anything about and suddenly realized why Anderson was charging manslaughter. He didn't know much about the nuances of the law, but he was pretty sure anything more than that would have been open to reasonable doubt. Perry Mason, of course, would have used the reasonable doubt angle. Maybe he could do the same. Considering Tom's lack of trial experience, Perry was about all he had to go on. He thought he would try that tack. "But, Your Honor, I only have experience with one murder trial."

The judge nodded. "That's why Mr. Thornton will act as co-counsel. But we all saw what you did the other day. You're a natural-born defense attorney, son."

Glancing over at Anderson, he noticed the state's attorney was nodding while also avoiding Tom's gaze.

He looked over at Johnson who was watching him closely. With a sigh, Tom said, "Well, Mr. Johnson, you're the one on trial. What do you think?"

Johnson shrugged. "I know you're as green as they come, but you sure as hell got Howie Kirkpatrick off without even breaking a sweat."

The man's cavalier attitude gave Tom the willies. Leland Johnson had murdered his own son. Everyone in that room knew that was true. The whole thing was like some kind of bizarre chess game they were all playing just to make everything look right.

He sat back in his chair and looked around the room one last time. In the end, his final thought was simple: everyone was entitled to a defense. Even Leland Johnson.

...

"Eugene Mayer appears to have suffered a stroke here in court, today," said Judge Frederick to the packed courtroom as soon as the bailiff called everyone to order.

After letting all the gasps and whispers die down, the judge looked at Leland Johnson who was sitting at the far end of the defense table. Tom was sitting on the other end and Mr. Thornton was in the middle. "Mr. Johnson, I hereby appoint Thomas Jarrell as your attorney with L.O. Thornton as his co-counsel."

More gasps and whispers. The judge banged his gavel a couple of times and then looked at Anderson. "Does the state have any objections to this course of action?"

Anderson halfway stood and said, "No, Your Honor," before resuming his seat.

"Mr. Jarrell, do you have any motions?"

Tom stood. "Yes, Your Honor. I request a continuance until Monday, October 6th." That would give him a solid week to prepare. He knew neither Anderson nor the judge would agree, but he wanted to make sure he at least made a show of getting as much time as he could.

Anderson stood. "The state objects, Your Honor. This jury has been impaneled for this trial and are ready to fulfill their civic duty. Any delay will possibly poison the pool and require a new jury, regardless."

The judge, who appeared to already have his mind made up, said, "I think we can give Mr. Jarrell a continuance until Wednesday."

Anderson didn't reply.

The judge made a downward waving motion with his hands. Tom didn't understand what he meant until he saw Anderson sit down. Tom did the same.

Turning to the jury, Judge Frederick said, "Ladies and gentlemen, I am granting a continuance of two days to the defense. This means that you are dismissed for this afternoon, but you are required to report back on Wednesday morning at 9 a.m. During this time, you are to ignore any news reports about this trial. Likewise, you are to refrain from discussing this trial with anyone outside of this courtroom." He frowned. Tom had always heard that Judge Frederick was a tyrant of a father. He was a fair judge, or that had been Tom's experience up until that morning. He had the sneaking suspicion that the judge was railroading Leland Johnson, but Johnson didn't seem to agree—he seemed to be satisfied, if not downright happy, with the turn of events. In any case, the judge, right then, looked like an angry father reprimanding his children. "Your failure to follow my instructions will require me to issue a warrant against you for contempt of court and the penalties are harsh, including jail time." He surveyed the jurors with his eyes. "Do you all understand?"

Tom watched closely as they all nodded, some looking defiant while others appeared to be a cowed.

"Very good." Turning back to Tom, the judge said, "Request for continuance granted until Wednesday, October 1st, at 9 a.m." He paused with his left eyebrow arched.

Tom said, "Thank you, Your Honor." He was sure there was something else he needed to ask for, but his mind was a blank. All he wanted to do was to get into a room with Leland Johnson and find out what strategy he and Mr. Mayer had cooked up.

"Court is adjourned until Wednesday." The judge banged his gavel and that was that.

...

Tom was meeting with Leland Johnson in the same room where they'd met with the judge just a few minutes earlier. Johnson was free on bail, of course, the charge only being manslaughter, or that was what Tom thought. That meant they could have met in Daytona Beach, but Tom wanted to get as much from the man as he could and as soon as he could.

Ronnie, who was obviously upset with him for taking the case, had reluctantly agreed to wait for him at The Sugar Bowl diner over on Woodland.

Mr. Thornton had suggested Tom meet with Johnson alone and that they (Mr. Thornton and Tom) meet first thing in the morning. That had been fine with Tom. He'd even suggested that Mr. Thornton come over to his office at 9 the next morning, something the old man had been more than happy to agree to, which made Tom wonder what, if anything, he would be able to help with. Mostly nothing was Tom's guess.

So, there he was, face to face with Leland Johnson, the man who'd murdered his own son and Howie's lover. And Johnson had a smirk on his face.

"Before we start, Tom, I want you to know I appreciate your help." If Marveen had been there, taking notes, Johnson's words would have read sincere on the typed page, but his voice was dripping with sarcasm as he slouched in his chair. "You don't like me, and I don't like you, but we're stuck with each other. To show you my appreciation, however, I wanna tell you about something that I'm sure you'll be interested to hear. In fact,"—he crossed his legs—"let's call this little nugget my fee. Agreed?"

Tom crossed his arms. "My fee in this case is the same as the one I charged for Howie's defense. One thousand dollars." Although he didn't think Johnson would have any way of knowing, that was how much his wife had paid Tom for defending Howie when she'd come by his office the previous Tuesday to give her affidavit before leaving town. She'd also handed him an additional four thousand to give to Howie however Tom thought best. Johnson most definitely did not need to know that.

At the mention of a thousand dollars, Johnson rolled his eyes. "Sure. And pigs flew that day. Ben Kirkpatrick never had money like that and neither did his fag son."

He smirked again. "But, nice try." He crossed his arms and shifted in his chair. "No, this nugget is worth a helluva lot more than a grand."

Tom figured he had nothing to lose. He doubted Johnson would ever pay him a penny, so he said, "What is it, then?"

"Well, Mayer told me this morning that his boys had found that dyke kid, Pauline, and her girlfriend and that he had put in a call to Pauline's father to let him know where you'd stashed them. At the New Cortez." His smirk turned into a grin. "He didn't have a chance to tell me whether or not my *business acquaintance, Mr. Roger G. Thompson, from Saint Augustine, Florida,* had driven down or not." He laughed to himself as he quoted his wife's affidavit.

Tom took in a deep breath and tried not to reveal the sudden fear that gripped him. And, as much as he wanted to sock the banker right in his smirking face, Tom managed to hold off. He had a passing thought about how that would be a perfect job for Ronnie and then cleared his throat to get back to the matters at hand. "You mentioned your wife is on her way back to Daytona Beach, what—"

Johnson sat up a little. "Damn right, that bitch of a wife of mine is on her way back to town. As you saw, no one knew about it, other than Mayer and myself. He was able to serve her with a subpoena and, being the idiot she is, she complied. Only thing is, her plane had engine trouble and, from what Mayer told me, was stuck in Charlotte last night. She should be arriving on the 4:45 this afternoon."

Tom thought about that for a moment. "Why didn't you want to say anything about it in chambers? Mr. Anderson was bound to find out. Mr. Mayer was obliged to tell him before the trial started."

Johnson sat all the way up. He leaned forward. "That was all Eugene Mayer and his courtroom tricks. I didn't and still don't give a fuck what anyone says to Mervyn Anderson. I know I'm in for it. Like I told Mayer, all I want is for you to make sure I get the minimum." He smirked at Tom. "I've sold the bank, already, to a buyer out of Jacksonville. I'm converting all my assets to cash. Once I get out of the big house, I'll be setting up shop in Cuba."

Tom had no idea what the minimum was for manslaughter. He figured it was a year. And, he could easily see Judge Frederick agreeing to that if there was enough reasonable doubt. He couldn't see the jury, however, finding Leland Johnson not guilty. That brought him to another question. "So, if Mrs. Johnson was on her way down, why did Mr. Mayer serve me with a subpoena?"

"You were plan B. If that bitch wouldn't cooperate, then he was gonna try and impeach you on the stand." Johnson offered him an evil smiled. "And, Mr. Jarrell, Eugene Mayer found out all about you and Ronnie Grisham."

Tom looked up at the ceiling. He was surprised he wasn't more afraid. He felt a kind of flat acceptance: *that was that*. As his mind rolled forward, he thought he might as well cash out and take Ronnie with him to some place like San Francisco. Mr. Mayer would recover from his stroke and be holding whatever he had over Tom's head for as long as the man lived. Leland Johnson, even in Cuba, would have endless amounts of blackmail material.

Then Tom had a thought. It was crazy and probably not true, but it was worth following up on. He looked over at Leland Johnson, right in the eyes, and asked, "What are you talking about?"

The man blinked and said, "How you and Grisham are, you know..."

Tom could feel his confidence growing. He crossed his arms. "No, Mr. Johnson, I don't know."

Johnson's bravado, and Tom was sure that was what it was, appeared to fade a bit. If he had the goods on Tom and Ronnie, he would have been gloating. Maybe Mr. Mayer had only hinted at something. Johnson sighed. "Well, all I know is what Eugene Mayer told me."

"What was that?" Tom tried his best to frown disapprovingly.

Johnson shrugged. "Something about you and Grisham being lovers."

Tom shook his head and sighed. "My wife just died, Mr. Johnson." He hoped that moved the man off the scent of the trail. For good measure, he added, "I can't believe I ever trusted Mr. Mayer."

Johnson slouched a little. "Me, neither. He screwed me, too."

"Oh?"

"Yeah. To help hide the fact that I've been selling off stocks and bonds, he set up a shell company to do the selling for me." Johnson frowned. "And, after first agreeing to a fee of ten percent, he kept fifty."

Tom nodded, feeling unreasonably gleeful. Mr. Mayer had nothing on him and Leland Johnson was getting screwed. He knew he shouldn't revel in another man's misery, but it was hard not to.

"You're enjoying this, aren't you?"

Tom shook his head. "Not really. I have a job to do and I'm going to do it. But I don't like tricks. What else did Mr. Mayer tell you about his plan for your defense?"

Johnson snorted and looked off to his left. "Not a

damn thing. All he had was his attempt to impeach Inez and, if she failed to show up, he was going after you." He looked right at Tom. "You have no idea how lucky you got today. I watched Mayer's eyes sparkle every time he talked about the fact that he was going to go after you when he got you on the stand. He's one vindictive son of a bitch. I think he was a little disappointed that Inez agreed to come down here for the trial."

Tom nodded and tried to look worried, but he doubted he was succeeding very well.

Chapter 10

On the Daytona Beach Highway
Monday, September 29, 1947
Later that afternoon

They were halfway to Daytona Beach by the time Tom finished his sordid little tale of those two sumbitches: Leland Johnson and Eugene Mayer.

It had been one hell of a roller-coaster that afternoon, starting with Mayer and his courtroom antics (Ronnie still wasn't convinced the lawyer hadn't induced himself into a stroke, somehow). After Judge Frederick had announced Tom would be representing sumbitch number one, Leland Johnson, Ronnie had nearly pitched a fit.

At first, he'd sat and stewed at the Sugar Bowl, angry that Tom had agreed to defend the man. He'd tried to convince himself that Judge Frederick had forced him to do it, but he knew Tom well enough to know that his lawyer's idea of how everyone deserves a defense had probably been the bottom line and that Tom wouldn't have put up much of a fight.

However, now that he knew what he knew, Ronnie was mighty relieved that things had taken the turn they had.

"So," said Tom from the passenger seat, his left hand on Ronnie's thigh, "The first thing to do is for us to head straight to the New Cortez and get Pauline and Bessie."

"We gotta stash them somewhere."

Tom nodded. "We can't put them up at our house. That's too obvious. What do you think?"

"How about we take them down to New Smyrna?"

"That sounds good."

"Or, better yet, give them a grand and put them on a plane for somewhere out of state?"

Tom looked at his watch. "It's too late to get that kind of money out of the bank."

"You really need to keep an emergency stash somewhere. You never know when the two of us might have to blow town. And it won't probably happen during banking hours."

Tom sighed. "You're right."

Ronnie knew he was right. He'd been thinking about just that very thing for a couple of days. They needed to put five grand, or maybe ten, in a briefcase and hide it. If things got bad, and there was always that possibility, they would have the cash to get out of town, and fast.

It was becoming more and more plainly obvious that being really and truly in love with Tom carried a certain price Ronnie had never considered. To have the kind of life they both seemed to want, they would have to be more careful. Ronnie had been thinking about that a lot over the last few days, ever since Miz Mabel had asked about why he wasn't sleeping over there. And that reminded him... "I still gotta go move my stuff out of Miz Mabel's."

Tom nodded. "Of course." He thought for a moment. "But we have to take care of Pauline and Bessie first." He sighed. "I wish I knew who Mayer hired to do his investigator work."

"Who did he use when you worked for him?"

"I don't know. He was always secretive about everything."

"Well, I could ask around..."

Tom shook his head. "It wouldn't be worth it."

"Are you sure Mayer doesn't have the goods on us?" Ronnie couldn't help worrying about that. He thought Tom was being a little too trusting of the fact that Leland Johnson had backed down.

"I don't know, to be honest. But let's cross that bridge when we get to it, OK?" He looked over at Ronnie who quickly glanced over and saw the little crease on his forehead. He reached across the seat and rubbed on it with his left thumb. He was pretty sure he would never, ever get tired of doing that.

...

As they drove into town, Tom asked Ronnie to quickly stop at the airport. He wanted to check the arrival of whichever flight it was that was coming in from Charlotte that Inez Johnson would be on. He guessed she would be coming in on Eastern, but he wasn't sure.

At the airport, Ronnie pulled up by the curb and said, "I'll keep the motor running. I have a bad feeling about those gals."

Tom nodded as he stepped out of the car. He turned and leaned back in. "I'll be right back." In a whisper, he added, "I love you, Ronnie Grisham." Because he did.

Giving him a big grin, his friend nodded. "Me too. Now, scoot."

Tom closed the Buick's door and ran into the terminal building. The Eastern desk was just inside, on the right. Just in front, there was a small cluster of three men huddled together, hats pushed back and hands on hips, all quietly talking. He saw a couple of women, one of whom looked to be in her 50s or 60s, sitting nearby, who were both crying into their handkerchiefs. He wondered what was going on.

As he walked up, a worried-looking man behind the desk hung up a telephone he'd been whispering into and, in a loud and projecting voice, said, "May I have your attention, ladies and gentlemen?" The terminal immediately went silent. "I have received confirmation from New York. I'm sorry to announce that Flight 653 did, in fact, crash upon take-off from Columbia, South Carolina. Local authorities have confirmed there were no survivors." The two women cried out. One of the men walked over and knelt down, holding the older woman's hand and talking to her as he did.

Tom walked up and, as often happened because of his height, the two other men stepped aside to let him by. He looked down at the clerk, whose face was ashen. He appeared to be slightly shaking. Tom took off his hat and said, "Excuse me."

Looking up, the clerk said, "Yes, sir?"

"Was that the flight that would have been coming in from Charlotte?"

"Yes, sir."

"Is there any way for me to find out if a specific person was on it?"

"I'm waiting for a wire with the passenger names. It could be an hour or so."

Tom asked, "Is there anyone I could call who would know now?"

The man frowned disapprovingly. "Well, I suppose you could call the Charlotte desk and ask if your..."

"Friend," added Tom quickly.

"You could ask if your friend got on the plane up there."

Nodding, Tom reached over and picked up a flight schedule from a small rack on the counter. "Is the number in here?"

The man looked relieved, as if he realized Tom wasn't asking him to do much more. "No. The numbers in there are for reservations. Your best bet is to call person-to-person and ask for the Eastern desk at the Charlotte airport."

Tom tried to smile. "Thank you. And, I'm sorry."

The man nodded. He looked over at the two women. "This is the first time something like this has happened since I started this job."

Tom tried to buoy his spirits. "If it helps, you're being very professional."

The man smiled blandly. "Thank you, sir."

. . .

Dropping a nickel in the first payphone he found, Tom waited for the operator.

"Number, please."

"3772."

"One moment."

After two rings, Marveen picked up. "Law offices of Tom Jarrell. May I help you?"

"Marveen, it's Mr. Jarrell."

"Hello, Mr. Jarrell. How did the trial go?"

"You haven't heard?"

"No, what?"

"Mr. Mayer had a stroke during his opening statement."

"Oh my!"

"I need you to do two things for me, please."

"Of course."

"First, call the Eastern Airlines desk at the airport in Charlotte, North Carolina, and find out if Inez Johnson was on their flight 653 today."

"What—?"

"No time to explain. You have that?"

She repeated everything back to him perfectly.

"Thank you. Then, I need you to call Pauline and Bessie and tell them to pack their bags and to be waiting for us when we get there. We're at the airport right now and headed straight for the New Cortez."

"They're here, Mr. Jarrell." He was pretty sure he heard Bessie giggling in the background.

"Oh? Why?"

"Bessie wanted to take a long walk so they did."

Tom tried to figure out what to do. They couldn't stay there. Finally, he said, "Do you have your car with you?"

"Yes, sir."

"Take them over to your house. Forget the call to Charlotte. Go over there right now." He had a thought. "Have the girls keep an eye out for anyone who might be following you. Mr. Johnson called Pauline's father and told him where they were. Hopefully, he's not down here yet."

"Oh, my!"

"Yes. Now, what is your address?"

"728 North Wild Olive. We're at the corner of Riverview."

"Ronnie and I will meet you there."

"Oh."

"Problem?"

"Well, there's Mother."

"Tell her the truth and let me deal with the consequences, if any. If she's anything like you, Marveen, I'm sure she'll come around."

"I hope so."

"Close up the office, get into your car, and get to your house. Go as fast as you can without breaking any laws. We'll be right behind you."

"OK."

. . .

Ronnie pulled Tom's Buick in right behind Marveen's DeSoto. He turned and looked at his pal with a big grin. "You ready to meet Mrs. Dodge?"

Tom shrugged as he opened his door. "As ready as I'll ever be, I suppose."

Ronnie laughed at that and followed Tom across the lawn and up to the front door. The door was open, but the screen was locked. Ronnie could hear Marveen saying, "Mother! You're not serious, are you?"

An older woman replied, "I am. They just announced it over WMFJ before you got here."

Tom knocked on the screen door.

After a few seconds, Marveen appeared, arms folded and looking angry. "Is it true?"

Ronnie watched as Tom slumped a little. Instead of answering, he asked, "May we come in?"

"I don't know, Mr. Jarrell. I'm not in the habit of entertaining men who defend murderers."

Ronnie, without thinking about it too much, said, "Well, you better quit right now, Marveen. This ain't gonna be the last one Tom defends."

Before anyone else could say anything, an older woman wearing steel glasses appeared behind Marveen. "For heaven's sake, y'all come in before the neighbors start listening in."

Marveen reluctantly unlatched the door and disappeared behind the older woman who pushed it open and, offering a smile, said, "I'm Mrs. Eugenia Dodge and I'm pleased to meet you both."

Tom ducked in, saying, "Nice to meet you, Mrs. Dodge. I'm—"

"I know who you are. Come in and let's get this door closed."

. . .

Marveen sighed. Mr. Jarrell had been right. Her mother had barely batted an eye when she'd shown up with Pauline and Bessie in tow. Now they were all sitting around in her mother's living room, right in front of a photograph of her father in his sergeant's uniform, and talking about how to make sure the girls didn't end up in Chattahoochee and how to defend a murderer. She wondered what her daddy would have made of it all.

Mr. Jarrell had explained how it wasn't really his choice to defend that awful Leland Johnson, but she was having a hard time convincing herself that she could get through the next few days knowing she would be helping a murderer be set free. If there was one thing she knew, it was that Mr. Tom Jarrell was smart and, if anyone could get Leland Johnson off, it would be him.

Mr. Jarrell looked at Ronnie Grisham and asked about his going over to the New Cortez and checking whether anyone had been snooping around asking for Pauline or Bessie. Ever since Mr. Jarrell had admitted the truth about the two of them, Marveen found herself watching them closely to see if she could find any hint of what two men in love with each other looked like.

What she'd mostly come to realize was they both were doing just what Mr. Jarrell said he wanted and keeping their conversations professional. If anything, Marveen had slowly begun to think of them as an old married couple. After all, hadn't they known each other since all the way back in 1935? That was over 12 years.

Then, as she often did, she remembered Mrs. Jarrell and Missy and got confused again.

Realizing she'd lost track of the conversation, she decided to pay attention to what was going on in her mother's living room. Right then, Pauline was talking. "But, Mr. Jarrell, I'm an adult."

"How old are you?"

"I just turned 20."

Mr. Jarrell sighed. "Well, the law isn't exactly clear about all of this. For some things, you're an adult at 18. For others, you have to be 21. But..." He hesitated, that little crease forming in his forehead as he frowned. "In certain matters, many judges will defer to your father since you're not married."

Bessie exclaimed, "That's just not fair!"

Mr. Jarrell and her mother both nodded. Her mother said, "It's not fair but it's how things are." She then turned to Mr. Jarrell and, with one of her long sighs, said, "Of course, there's an easy way out of all this."

Marveen saw Ronnie break into one of his silly grins as he elbowed Mr. Jarrell. "I know what she's gonna say and I don't disagree."

Like Mr. Jarrell, Marveen was completely confused and said as much.

Her mother looked at her reprovingly. "They should marry each other."

Marveen couldn't believe her mother would suggest such a thing. It was impossible! "Two women can't get married."

Her mother rolled her eyes. One day, thought Marveen, those eyes were going to fall out and drop right on the floor. "No, Marveen—"

Ronnie jumped right in. "We should marry Pauline and Bessie."

Marveen looked over at the two girls, both of whom looked like they had just bit into a lemon.

Mr. Jarrell nodded thoughtfully. "It would solve a lot of problems, that's for sure."

Bessie vigorously shook her head. "Absolutely not!"

Ronnie got down on his left knee in front of Bessie and held out his right hand. "Come on, Bessie, woncha please marry me? I make a solemn vow to never kiss you 'cept to convince the judge it's the real thing and I promise you half my worldly goods, which, right now, is half of about seventeen bucks."

With that, the two girls exchanged looks and then burst out laughing.

Chapter 11

Driving north on U.S. Route 1
Folkston, Ga.
Monday, September 29, 1947
Half past 7 in the evening

Tom sighed. They were about 30 miles south of Waycross, having just crossed the Florida-Georgia line a few minutes earlier. That was when he and Ronnie had likely violated the Mann Act by transporting Pauline and Bessie across a state line for "immoral purposes."

Ronnie, who was driving Tom's Buick and way too fast for Tom's comfort, reached over and patted Tom's cheek. "Stop worryin', bud."

From the backseat, Bessie said, "I promise you, Mr. Jarrell, this is going to work. I know about all about Judge Perkins and, well, I don't think we'll have any trouble."

Pauline added, "And, I don't know how to thank you enough, Mr. Jarrell."

Ronnie said, "Just don't kiss him, except when the judge says you have to."

Bessie and Pauline both giggled while Tom sighed again and looked out the window in the fading light of dusk.

. . .

Ronnie figured the problem was that Tom was worrying about the Mann Act. He looked over at his pal who was staring out at the passing cotton fields, the puffy white bolls glowing eerily in the sunset.

Ronnie, however, felt like he was betraying Sarah. Tom had no idea, but it had been Ronnie who'd convinced Sarah to say yes back in 1939 when Tom had proposed. And, it was Ronnie who'd suggested to Tom that he and Sarah should get hitched in the first place. The whole thing had been his idea.

Ronnie could see the writing on the wall back then. He knew that, once Tom entered law school later that fall at Stetson in DeLand, it would look funny if he didn't at least have a girlfriend. And, truth be told, Mrs. Jarrell, Tom's mother, had been talking to Ronnie pretty much non-stop about how worried she was that Tom didn't seem to have much interest in Sarah even though they'd known each other for a couple of years and, supposedly, been going together that whole time.

Mrs. Jarrell had first met Sarah at the Teachers' College in Tallahassee and told her all about her handsome son at the university in Gainesville who was so tall, even though neither she nor Mr. Jarrell had any history of tall ancestors that either one knew of.

As they got closer to Waycross, Ronnie felt as if all their ghosts were crowded in the car with Tom, Pauline, Bessie, and himself.

He could easily see Mr. Jarrell. He was worried with that same crease in his forehead that, even though he only stood 5'9", definitely meant he was Tom's father. He wouldn't have said anything. He would have just sat there and stared at the rest of them, looking like he thought they were all crazy.

Mrs. Jarrell, however, would be glancing around the car with her left hand over her mouth (whenever Marveen did that, Ronnie always thought of Tom's mother) and would be saying to anyone who would listen, "Well, I just don't know. I don't understand any of this but, if Tommy says it's right, then it must be right. No one I've ever met was ever as smart as my Tommy." Ronnie grinned at that thought. He agreed with her a thousand percent.

But, what about Sarah? What would she say? As if she was sitting between the two of them on the front seat, something she'd done plenty of times back in DeLand before Tom went off to the war, Ronnie could hear her saying, "Well, of course you two should marry these girls. It only makes sense and I don't understand what you're worrying about. This queer judge in Waycross will take care of it all and that will be that."

...

Judge Arnold Perkins lived on a quiet street at the edge of Waycross, about ten minutes' drive from Route 1. Ronnie had stopped at a Pure filling station and asked for directions when they crossed the city limits.

Tom pressed the doorbell, secretly hoping he wasn't in.

But, after a few seconds, the porch light turned on and the front door creaked opened. An older man in a tied-up flannel robe peered out into the night through the screen door. "Yes?"

Bessie quickly stepped forward. "Judge Perkins?"

"Yes?"

"It's me, Elizabeth Newkirk."

The man suddenly smiled. "Bessie! Dear child! What are you doing here?"

"May we come in?"

The judge unlatched the screen and stepped back to let them in. "Of course, of course."

Once they were all inside, the man looked Tom and Ronnie up and down with a slightly lecherous smile. "And who are your handsome friends?"

Bessie took the judge by the arm and led him into an old-fashioned parlor, complete with gas bulb lamps that were lit and burning. "Judge Perkins, I have a problem and you're the only one who can solve it."

Pauline followed the two of them. Tom and Ronnie brought up the rear.

. . .

Bessie finished her story by saying, "And, so, the only solution we can come up with is for Mr. Grisham to marry me and for Mr. Jarrell to marry Pauline."

The judge, who was sitting on a red velvet love seat by himself looked over at Ronnie with interest. "And you are Mr. Grisham?"

Tom watched with amusement as Ronnie nodded, suddenly blushing as he did. "Yes, sir."

Turning to Tom, he said, "I seem to have heard your name recently. Why?"

Pauline jumped in. "He was involved in a murder trial in Daytona Beach. He's a lawyer who got his client off."

The judge nodded. "Of course. Your client was Howard Kilpatrick?"

"Kirkpatrick," corrected Tom quietly.

Waving his hand in the air, the judge said, "Oh, yes. Such a handsome lad." With a small grin, he asked, "Was it the case, as some have said, that it was his *boyfriend* who was murdered? And by the boy's own father?"

Tom nodded. "Yes, sir."

The judge shook his head. "Such intolerance! So little respect for the natural course of love." He made a tut-tut sound with his tongue. Looking around the room, he said, "Well, of course, these marriages must be performed and tonight. I *absolutely* see the exigency and will gladly waive the requirements for blood tests and a waiting period." He looked at Bessie fondly. "Chattahoochee is no place for two young ladies as pretty and as sweet as yourselves."

Pauline smiled while Bessie giggled at that and said, "Thank you, Judge Perkins. I knew you would understand."

The man nodded and then looked at Ronnie. Standing, he said, "Now, as for my fee..."

Tom pulled out his wallet. "How much, Your Honor?"

Walking over to Tom, the judge suddenly leaned over and kissed him on the forehead. It took Tom by surprise. "Oh no, silly boy. I don't think you *quite* understand."

Before he knew what was happening, he saw Ronnie standing next to the judge, looming above him by a good foot or so. "Your Honor?" Ronnie politely held out his arm.

The judge inserted his hand into the crook of Ronnie's elbow. "Thank you, young man. So polite." With a wink, the older man said to Tom. "Don't worry, Mr. Jarrell. We'll only be a few minutes. You see, I am a student of human anatomy and I'm sure your friend has *certain* physical attributes that are *quite* unique. Once

I've had a few moments to *study* them and make sure they offer no *impediment* to marriage, we'll be right back and I'll gladly perform the *solemn* rite of marriage."

Tom watched, not sure whether to laugh or not, as the judge led Ronnie up the stairs. Once they made it to the landing on the second floor, Tom heard the judge say, "In here, Mr. Grisham."

...

Handing out the marriage certificates to Ronnie and Tom, the judge said, "Well, that's that, my children. You may certainly skip any unnecessary kissing." He winked up at Tom. "However, if you would like to kiss your husband..." He then turned to Pauline. "And your wife..."

Ronnie and Pauline switched places with a laugh. Taking Tom into his arms, he planted his lips on his pal's and kissed him long and hard. He only stopped when the judge cleared his throat.

"Well, well, I see it is that time," said the judge. "I really do *need* my beauty sleep."

The four of them laughed at that and headed towards the front door. Behind him, Ronnie heard Tom say, "In all seriousness, Your Honor, I do feel like I should pay you a fee."

"Well, if it will make you feel better, I'll take ten dollars. Five each."

As Ronnie waited by the door, he watched Tom pull out his wallet and hand the judge a ten. Then, to his surprise, Tom leaned over and kissed the judge on the forehead. "Thank you, Your Honor."

The judge turned red and put his hand on his chest. "My, my, Mr. Jarrell, this is so sudden!" Turning to Ronnie, the old man winked and said, "What will your husband think of me?"

They all laughed and, as they made their way onto the porch, the judge said, "Do take care of yourselves, my dears. And visit anytime."

Bessie turned and kissed the judge on the cheek. "Thank you, Judge Perkins. You're a lifesaver."

The old man nodded, put his hand on her cheek, and said, "A pleasure, my dear. I am so glad you are now safe." He looked at Pauline and pointed. "You take good care of my Bessie. Do you hear me?"

They all laughed again as Pauline said, "Yes, sir. I promise, Your Honor."

. . .

Once they were across the state line, Tom looked over at Ronnie. "Well, what, exactly was the fee?"

Bessie sat forward eagerly. "Yes! Did he make you do unnatural things?"

Ronnie kept his eyes on the road and laughed. "A gentleman never tells."

Pauline said, "Come on, now!"

With a big grin, Ronnie shrugged and said, "Well, if you really wanna know..."

"We do, we do," clamored the gals in the back.

Tom added. "Yes, we do." He then turned and looked over the back of the seat. "And when Ronnie's done, it'll be your turn, Bessie. I want to know all about Judge Perkins."

Ronnie heard her giggle and then say, "That's fine, Mr. Jarrell."

"Tom."

She giggled again. "That's fine, Tom. Fair is fair."

Ronnie said, "Well, the judge led me by the hand into a bedroom with a huge four-poster bed..."

"Yes?" said Bessie, breathlessly.

"He then told me to remove my coat, unbutton my shirt, and drop my trousers..."

"Yes?" said Tom with a chuckle.

"Then he pulled over a stool and I helped him get up on it. He made me pose like they do in the magazines..."

"Yes?" said Pauline with a giggle.

"Then he felt up my muscles and..."

"And what?" asked Bessie, her voice pitched up high right behind him.

"He looked inside my drawers and..."

"And then what?" asked Tom with another chuckle.

"And then he fainted when he saw what was in there."

The two girls squealed and groaned with both delight and disgust in the back seat while Tom reached over and patted that very thing, whispering, "Of course he did."

Chapter 12

New Cortez Hotel
800 N. Atlantic Avenue
Daytona Beach, Fla.
Monday, September 29, 1947
Half past 11 in the evening

Tom walked up to the front desk with Pauline on his arm. "I'd like a room for a week, please." Ronnie and Bessie had followed them into the hotel lobby and were standing behind them.

The woman sitting on a stool at the counter, and looking like she was ready for bed, suddenly came to life. With a suspicious frown, she asked, "Dearie, aren't you in Room 219 with Miss Newkirk?" She looked around Pauline and took in Bessie and Ronnie with a scowl.

"Yes, ma'am, I was. But we just got married and my husband would like to take a room."

Tom admired how well she answered the question considering she was only 20.

"Married?" The woman looked over her glasses at Pauline. With a sickening smile, she asked, "Where's your ring, dearie?"

Tom smiled down at the woman. "It was all of a sudden. We'll be getting a ring tomorrow."

The woman shook her head. "I know you, Mr. Jarrell. Shame on you, your wife and daughter dead just a few months, and this girl barely of age." Crossing her arms, she said, "Sorry, I don't rent rooms to unmarried couples."

Tom pulled the marriage certificate out of his coat pocket and handed it over. "Here's proof."

The woman took the paper and read it over. With a resigned sigh, she handed it back and said, "Fine. Sign here."

Tom leaned over the book and, as he signed, said, "Mr. and Mrs. Thomas Jarrell." He felt a sharp pang of regret. He suddenly wished he could take everything back. For as guilty as he sometimes felt with Ronnie in bed next to him at home, in the very spot where Sarah had once slept, he felt even worse signing his name like that again.

Pauline, sensing there was something wrong, leaned against him and whispered, "It's OK, Tom."

He nodded and patted her arm. "Thanks."

The woman behind the counter slapped down a key. "Room 207. Next."

Tom pulled Pauline to the side as Ronnie walked forward with Bessie on his arm. She brightly said, "Hello, Mrs. Kingston."

"License, please," snapped the older woman.

Ronnie pulled out his and handed it over. The woman shook her head as she quickly read it. "And, you, Ronnie Grisham." Handing it back and looking at Bessie, she added, "I hope you know what you've gotten yourself into, dearie."

Bessie giggled and replied, "I sure do."

"Sign here."

Ronnie leaned over and said, "Mr. and Mrs. Ronald Hoover Grisham," as he signed.

Pauline whispered, "Hoover?"

Tom chuckled and nodded. "Yes."

...

They gathered in Room 207 to share a bottle of champagne that Ronnie had stopped to buy when they were driving through Jacksonville. Using paper cups, Ronnie poured out some for each of them and then lifted up his cup. Looking at Bessie, he said, "Congratulations to my blushing bride, Mrs. Ronald Grisham."

Everyone laughed and had a sip.

Then Ronnie decided to add, "And to my blushing husband, Mr. Thomas Jarrell."

Bessie said, "Here, here!" as she sipped from her cup a second time. Ronnie winked at her and then looked at his pal.

Tom lifted his cup. His smile faded. "To my second wife, I apologize." He drained his cup.

Pauline looked down at the floor and didn't reply.

Ronnie said, "Sorry, Pauline."

Bessie walked over and hugged her girlfriend from the side. "Buck up, Paul."

No one said anything for a while as the sounds of the crashing waves outside the open door got louder with a sudden shift in the wind. Finally, Pauline lifted her cup. "To the first Mrs. Jarrell. Thanks for sharing your husband with me and Mr. Grisham, wherever you are." She drained her cup.

Ronnie said, "To Sarah," and drained his.

"To Sarah," echoed Bessie and emptied her cup as well.

Tom walked over and put his long hand on Pauline's shoulder. "Sorry about that."

The girl shook her curls and said, "No, I'm sorry we put you to all this trouble. We should have just gotten on a bus and headed out of state."

Tom sighed and looked out the door. "That would have only delayed things. This way, you two really are safe."

Ronnie, who, during the drive home had been thinking about all the ways being married to an actual woman would help both of them out, added, "And so are we, bud." Before he could help himself, he said, "And I think Sarah approves."

No one replied for a moment. Tom looked at his watch. "Well, I've still got a murdering asshole to defend, so we'd better go."

The two gals giggled as Pauline put her arm around Bessie. "And I need to remind my wife about all the ways we really are married, even if we don't have a piece of paper."

Ronnie put his hand on Tom's shoulder and added, "Ditto," with a wink.

Right then, Ronnie heard the sound of footsteps. Before anyone could do anything, two middle-aged men burst through the open door.

Pauline said, "Father!" while Bessie squeaked.

Tom pushed the two girls behind him. Ronnie jumped in front of Tom protectively, roughly asking, "Who are you and what do you want?"

The first man, slightly taller than the other, but still only reaching Ronnie's chin, said, "My name is Roger Thompson and that's my daughter, Pauline."

Ronnie grinned and patted Tom on the back. "Meet your new son-in-law, Mr. Thompson."

With a slack jaw, the man looked around the room. "What?"

From behind, Pauline said, "This *is* what you wanted, isn't it, Father? For me to get married?"

The man frowned. "Well, I wanted you to marry that Johnson boy." He looked up at Tom. "Not some scarecrow nobody."

"Hey!" said Ronnie with some heat. "Don't talk like that about the most famous lawyer in Volusia County, pops."

The man glanced at Ronnie. "And who are you?"

Looking over at the shorter man, who was also a little chubby, Ronnie replied, "Unless I'm mistaken, I'm this guy's new son-in-law."

The chubby man exploded. "Elizabeth! Is this true?"

"Yes, Daddy, it is. Ronnie and I just got married."

Mr. Thompson looked at Tom. "Is this all true, young man?"

"Yes, sir. Pauline and I were married in Georgia tonight."

"Judge Perkins!" exclaimed the chubby man.

Bessie didn't say anything.

"Look, Roger," said the chubby man to Mr. Thompson. "I know the judge who married them and he's as nutty as they come. We can get an annulment, easy."

Tom shook his head. "I don't think so, Mr. Newkirk. As your new son-in-law just said, I'm an attorney and I promise you no court in Georgia will annul either marriage."

No one said anything for a moment. Finally, Mr. Thompson, in a pleading voice, said, "Pauline, honey, you're sick. All I want is for you to get the help you need."

Tom crossed his arms. "Your daughter is not sick."

"Stay out of it," retorted Mr. Thompson. "This is a family matter."

Looking down, Tom said, "You're right. It is a family matter and I'm Pauline's family now. So, I'll kindly ask you to vacate the premises unless you want me to call the police and have you removed."

Ronnie grinned in spite of the tension in the room. He loved to see Tom be all lawyer-like. It always gave him a thrill.

Mr. Thompson considered the matter and then looked around Tom. "Pauline, I love you and your mother loves you. Won't you come home, pumpkin?"

"I'm sorry, Father," replied Pauline with a slightly quivering voice. "Like Tom said, *this* is my family."

Ronnie knew she was referring to the four of them and that made him feel real good and real proud. He also knew that, when it came to muscle, he was the one in charge of their little group, so he moved in slightly and said, "Mr. Thompson, Mr. Newkirk, if you don't mind..." He was careful not to touch either man as he used his bulk to clearly broadcast the message that it was time for them to leave. And, with only a little bit of grumbling, leave they did.

Chapter 13

106A N. Beach Street
Tuesday, September 30, 1947
Just before 9 in the morning

Tom walked into the office where he found Marveen already at her desk, smiling over a cup of coffee. "Did you see Bill last night?" was the obvious question.

Marveen nodded, her smile widening. "Yes, sir."

Tom smiled. "I'm glad to hear that." He had a sudden thought. "I hope you remembered—"

Marveen quickly interrupted him as she stood and walked over to the percolator. "Bill was the one who said that conversations about work, his or mine, are off limits."

"Good."

"So, Mr. Jarrell..." She handed him a mug of coffee.

"Yes, we all got married last night."

"And?" asked Marveen with a twinkle in her eyes.

Tom shrugged and took a sip of his coffee. "All I'll say

about *that* is that the right people were in bed with the right people this morning."

Marveen's left hand covered her mouth as she giggled.

He smiled over his coffee and then added, "And, please tell your mother that her timing was perfect. My father-in-law and Ronnie's father-in-law showed up right after we checked into the hotel."

"Hotel?"

Tom nodded. "I thought it would be best if Ronnie and I both registered at the New Cortzez as being married. That should get the gossip mills turning."

Marveen giggled again. "Did Eunice Kingston check you in?"

"She did. And she was none too happy about it. Wanted to see our marriage certificates and everything."

Nodding over her coffee, Marveen said, "Then most everyone beachside knows you're married by now."

Right then, there was a knock on the exterior door.

Tom looked at his watch. It was 9 on the dot. L.O. Thornton was right on time, which was no surprise.

...

"This is all I could find in Mayer's files." Mr. Thornton handed Tom a folder across his desk. Opening it, Tom found a certified transcript of the amicus brief and attached affidavit he'd filed the previous Wednesday.

Looking up, Tom asked, "Do you have any advice for me?"

The older man leaned back and then looked out the window. "You certainly do have a better view from your office than Mayer and myself." He cleared this throat. "And much better than your old cubby hole of an office."

Tom nodded with a smile and waited for Mr. Thornton to say something of substance.

Finally: "Well, my boy, I don't have much to offer. Criminal defense is Mayer's bailiwick." He crossed his spindly legs. "Anderson has charged manslaughter." It was a statement, not a question.

"Yes, sir."

Nodding for a moment, Mr. Thornton said, "Minimum is one year." He pursed his lips together. "Florida Farm number one up at Raiford can be something like a holiday with enough cash and knowing the right people. Or so I've heard." He rocked a little in the chair and then added, "Of course, the facility is properly segregated but there is a significant amount of intermingling with colored, something your client won't much care for."

Tom nodded. He suspected Leland Johnson was as much of a racist as he was anything else. "What do you know about his plans to relocate to Cuba after he finishes his sentence?"

Mr. Thornton raised his left eyebrow. "Did he tell you that?"

"Yes, sir. He sold the bank and Mr. Mayer was helping him sell his stocks and bonds. I don't plan to participate in any of that, myself."

Mr. Thornton was quiet for a moment before saying, "We don't always get to choose our clients... or our partners." He looked out the window again. "Very wise of you not to take Mayer up on his job offer. He was out to ruin you, Thomas."

Tom leaned forward. "And what about you, Mr. Thornton?"

Turning with a smile. "What about me in what regard?"

"Are you out to ruin me?"

His smile widened and seemed authentic. "I will admit I'm somewhat frightened by your brilliance and the fact that you don't quite know how smart you are but, no, Thomas, I have no desire to ruin anyone. I'm a wills and real estate kind of lawyer. Mayer is the shark. He's the litigator." Mr. Thornton sighed. "Did you know I'm fifteen years older than Mayer?"

Tom shook his head. He had no idea how much older either man was. "No, sir."

"Well, I am, and my doctor tells me I'll live another 20 years." He looked down and brushed some lint from his trouser leg. "Not that I care to, but it's nice to know I'll just go to sleep some night and not wake up." He cleared his throat. "Better than to make a fool of myself and pass out in open court." Tom was surprised at how bitter Mr. Thornton sounded.

"Have you heard how Mr. Mayer is doing?"

"No," was his short and direct answer. Having never seen any hint of it before, Tom was surprised to see the bitterness in the man's face.

Neither man said anything for a moment. Through the open window, Tom could hear pedestrians talking on the street below and some sea gulls talking to each other somewhere nearby.

Then Mr. Thornton said, "I notice you don't take notes."

"No, sir."

"Very odd to be a lawyer who doesn't take notes."

Tom smiled. "It interferes with my thinking." That was the excuse he'd used before.

"I suppose you have a photographic memory."

"No, sir. I just remember things." He then added, "Maybe I should take notes, now that I'm getting busier."

I wouldn't, Thomas." He suddenly stood.

Tom did the same.

With a smile, he said, "Good luck, young man."

"Thank you, Mr. Thornton."

"Of course."

The man turned and opened the office door. He then tipped his hat to Marveen as he walked by her desk and made his exit.

Tom stood there, a little bit in shock. He wasn't expecting much help, but he couldn't believe Mr. Thornton had left like that, as if he had somewhere better to be, leaving Tom high and dry, more or less.

...

Ronnie walked up to the little shack that sat between the marina and the shipyard. He knocked on the door and then waited. After a moment, a short man with almost no hair opened and looked up. "Yeah?"

With a grin, Ronnie said, "Remember me, Mr. Thomas?"

The man nodded but didn't reply.

"I need you to come back with me to court tomorrow."

"For what?"

"Mr. Jarrell wants you on the stand."

The man frowned. "Lemme see. Last time it was so I could go and testify that Mr. Johnson and someone I thought might be Skipper had taken Skipper's boat out on that Sunday night."

Ronnie nodded. "That's right."

"But I heard on the radio yesterday that Mr. Jarrell is now representin' Leland Johnson. So why would he want me?"

Ronnie shrugged with a grin. "I dunno. I'm not that smart."

Willy Thomas ran his bony hand over his chin and looked out at the river. "Well, sir, I think I'll take a pass this time. I can't see no good comin' outta this."

Ronnie spread his legs. "You know what a subpoena is?"

"Sure."

"Well, I'll be back this afternoon with one."

"You gotta find me to serve me with one, young man."

Ronnie shrugged.

Without saying anything else, the man walked back into the shack and slammed the door.

...

Tom shook his head as Ronnie wrapped up his reports from the morning. They were standing in front of Marveen's desk so she could hear everything as well. He said, "I should have sent you out with subpoenas."

Ronnie nodded. "Probably. But this is a new thing for both of us."

Tom looked down at Marveen and asked, "Do you have a form for a subpoena?"

She nodded. "There was one in that bunch of forms that Wanda sent over from Mr. Jordan's office in DeLand."

Tom put his hands on his hips. "I didn't see one in what I brought you last week."

She smiled. "I called Wanda to thank her last Thursday and she said she'd typed up a bunch more for me. They got here on Monday morning."

Ronnie looked at Tom. "You should send her some flowers."

Tom nodded and asked Marveen, "Will you take care of that?"

"Of course." She scribbled something on a notepad. Looking up, she asked, "Who gets subpoenas?"

. . .

Tom had his feet up on his desk as he read through the trial part of the newest Perry Mason: *The Case of the Fan-Dancer's Horse*. Marveen had picked it up for him from the library that morning. It had been out earlier in the month when he'd checked out the others. Unfortunately, there was nothing in the book about how to defend a client you didn't like.

As he read, he heard Ronnie say to Marveen, "I'm gonna take Tom out to lunch. You want us to bring you anything?"

"No, thanks. I'm going to meet your wife and her girlfriend at the house. Mother's made some Brunswick stew and I thought I'd save my pennies and go home for lunch."

As Tom smiled to himself, Ronnie laughed and said, "Tell Mrs. Grisham hello for me, if you would."

"Sure," replied Marveen.

Tom tried to get back into Perry's cross-examination of an obviously lying witness.

"You're taking all of this much better than I thought you would." That got Tom's attention. Ronnie was using his conciliatory voice, which wasn't something he used very often and was damn attractive when he did.

Marveen didn't immediately reply. After a moment, she said, "I'm doing the best I can with all this topsy-turvy stuff."

Looking through his office door, Tom saw Ronnie walk around to the right side of Marveen's desk and get on his haunches so he could look her in the eye. "I know it must all be so weird for you, Marveen. But I'm dang happy you're here, working with us, and I hope you'll stay on for a long time..." He paused. "Even after you marry Bill Gordon."

Marveen gasped. "What do you mean?"

As Tom watched, Ronnie leaned forward and kissed Marveen. "I know you're in love with him and I couldn't be happier for you."

"Thank you, Ronnie. That means a lot to me."

Ronnie leaned against her desk and stood. He looked over at Tom and winked. Turning back to Marveen, he patted his shirt pocket and added, "Even if he is just a little bit of a guy I could carry in my pocket."

Tom laughed out loud as Marveen indignantly exclaimed, "Ronnie Grisham!"

Chapter 14

761 S. Palmetto Avenue
Wednesday, October 1, 1947
Half past 6 in the morning

Alice walked into the kitchen and surprised Mr. Ronnie, who was standing there in just his underpants. He turned and looked at her with that big grin of his and said, "Wasn't expectin' you this early."

Alice looked around him and asked, "What are you doing to Mr. Tom's percolator?"

With as red a face as she'd ever seen on a white man, Mr. Ronnie said, "I'm tryin' to make coffee. But I haven't made my own in a long time. And never with a percolator."

Alice nodded and smiled. "Love will do strange things to a person."

He laughed. "You got that right."

"Well, Mr. Ronnie, why don't you go put some clothes on and let me take care of things in here?"

He nodded. "Yes, ma'am." With that, he ran out of the room.

As she cleaned up his mess, she shook her head. She was rarely attracted to a man's body, but she had to admit Mr. Ronnie had some great legs. They were covered in brown hair and all the muscles stood out.

To get that image out of her mind, she decided to think about how she and Betsy had made love over Saturday night. Her Aunt Mary had been unexpectedly called out of town, joining a group of volunteers from the N.A.A.C.P. who had headed to an emergency meeting in Sarasota. They'd traveled by private automobile, of course, and returned late on Sunday night. That had left Alice and Betsy alone for an entire night and day and they'd made the most of it, that was for sure.

. . .

"Alice is here," whispered Ronnie into Tom's ear.

"Huh?" Tom was in that twilight zone between being asleep and being awake. He wasn't sure what Ronnie had just said.

"Alice caught me in my drawers, trying to make coffee for you on your big day."

Tom sat up, panicked. "Alice is here? What time is it?"

"Relax, bud," said Ronnie soothingly. "It's only 6:30."

"Why is she here this early?"

"She probably had the same idea I did. You need a good breakfast before we drive over to DeLand."

Tom stretched and then leaned over and kissed Ronnie on the lips.

. . .

"Mr. Tom?"

"Yes, Alice?"

"Do you know anything about this Aaron Quince murder trial?"

"Some. Why?"

"Says here in the paper that the County Commissioners are going to impanel a new jury so that it includes colored folks. Does that affect your jury?"

Tom leaned over and looked at the front page of the paper. He quickly scanned the story and then appeared to relax. "That's for the Grand Jury. They're the ones who decide whether to issue an indictment."

"Why didn't Anderson send Skipper's case to the Grand Jury?" asked Ronnie as he spread some of Alice's peach jam on his toast.

"You'd have to ask him. There are a lot of questions around the Quince case, from what I've read."

"There sure are," said Alice over her coffee.

Ronnie looked at her. "What's the word over on Second Avenue?"

"There's a few who think he murdered that white woman in Holly Hill, but most question whether he can get a fair trial, regardless."

Tom nodded. "I'm worried about that too. I was glad to see that a new Grand Jury is being called. That should be fairer."

Alice put her cup down on the kitchen table. "What would be fair would be a Negro judge and a Negro State's Attorney and a Negro defense lawyer."

Ronnie asked, "Should there be a special colored-only court?"

Alice shrugged. "Why not? There's already a special whites-only court. Why can't a colored person get the same thing?" She looked up at Tom. "Didn't the Supreme Court say that we were to be treated equal in *Plessy*?"

Tom smiled a little and nodded. "They sure did. But I

don't think Mr. Justice Brown would have gone as far as that."

"*Plessy* is an abomination," said Alice without any heat but, from what Ronnie could tell, a lot of conviction.

Tom nodded. "You won't get any argument from me on that." He looked at her. "You really should be teaching school, Alice. Why don't you go somewhere up north where you could?"

She stood abruptly and put her cup in the sink. After a long moment of silence, she said in a thick voice, "Because, even up north, inverts can't teach school."

Tom sighed. "You're right. I'm sorry for bringing it up, Alice."

"Don't be, Mr. Tom." Ronnie watched as she grabbed a cup towel and wiped her face. "I appreciate the fact that you think I should be teaching school. I sometimes worry that my brain will turn to mush if I don't keep reading and doing the crosswords and anything I can to keep learning." She sighed. "Dr. Bethune is a big believer in lifelong learning."

"Me too," said Tom, the crease in his forehead getting deeper. Ronnie reached over and tried to erase it with his thumb as Tom smiled at him.

...

"Well, bud, are you ready?"

Tom looked out the window at the passing landscape. "As much as I will be."

"You got this, bud. I know it."

Tom sighed and began to recite his opening statement in his mind for what seemed like the three hundredth time.

...

"I feel like there is something I'm forgetting."

Ronnie looked over at his pal as they walked up the front steps of the courthouse. "I checked your briefcase before we left. Everything you talked about was in there."

Tom stopped at the top of the steps. Ronnie gently pushed him to the side to get him out of the way of the traffic of people coming to see Leland Johnson get his due. Ronnie noticed most of them would start to whisper when they realized Tom was standing there.

"What was it?" said Tom to himself as he looked out into space.

"There wasn't much, bud. But we got it all."

Tom shook his head. "Seems like it was something obvious."

"Well, I did try to serve those subpoenas yesterday..."

"No, that wasn't it." Tom was still shaking his head.

"You remember your opening statement, right?"

"Yes."

"Well, I think you're all set." Ronnie lowered his voice so no one would hear him. "All we need now is your asshole of a client."

Tom's face suddenly drained of all color. He turned and looked at Ronnie, the crease diving deep into his forehead. "Holy hell," he whispered.

"What?" asked Ronnie, feeling as alarmed as Tom looked.

"I never went over yesterday to see Leland Johnson."

Ronnie shrugged. "So? He told you everything there was to tell here on Monday."

Tom, still pale, whispered, "I never went to see him."

"So? I don't understand, bud."

Tom leaned in and gripped Ronnie's right coat lapel with his left hand. "What if he skipped?"

Ronnie laughed. "I hope to God he has."

. . .

"Mr. Jarrell, what do you have to say about all this?" Judge Frederick's face was splotchy, a clear indication he was angry.

Tom was still trying to recover from the news. He looked over at Sheriff Littlefield, who had just reported that his deputy found the Johnson house on Halifax empty. "Have you—?"

The judge slammed his hand on his desk. "Mr. Jarrell, Leland Johnson is your client!"

Tom leaned forward. He felt like he was on a slow-moving train that suddenly started careening out of control. "Your Honor, I—"

"So, you don't know where Mr. Johnson is?"

Tom shook his head. "No, Your Honor."

"And why shouldn't I hold you in contempt?"

Tom looked around the room. Mervyn Anderson, once again, was avoiding his gaze. Sheriff Littlefield, standing next to the judge's desk, was looking up at the ceiling. L.O. Thornton was nowhere to be found.

Taking a deep breath, Tom tried to find a thread of thought that made sense. Having nothing else to go on, he looked at Anderson and asked, "Is Mr. Johnson out on bond?"

Anderson closed his eyes as Judge Frederick exploded. "No, Mr. Jarrell, he is not! He is out on his own recognizance."

Tom, finally back to himself, turned and looked at the judge right in the eye. "Well, Your Honor, I didn't petition for my client to be released, so I'm not sure I can help you."

Anderson made a gurgling noise at that. The sheriff grinned as he kept his eyes on the ceiling. Judge Frederick stared at Tom for a long, piercing, burning moment.

After what seemed like forever, the judge calmly said, "Well, what's done is done. Mr. Jarrell, I suggest you work with the sheriff to locate your client. Otherwise, I'll be sentencing you to ten days for contempt."

Tom opened his mouth and then closed it. For some strange reason, it made him think of Marveen and how she did the same thing when she was flummoxed.

Anderson stirred in his seat and said, "Your Honor, I don't think—"

The judge held up his hand. "Don't talk to me, Merv. Between this case and the Quince case, you're up to your eyeballs in shit of your own making." His voice was getting louder. "All I'm doin' here is tryin' to get the only man I know who can get anythin' done to fuckin' do somethin'!" By that time, the judge was hollering and turning purple.

Sheriff Littlefield motioned to Tom with his right hand. "Come on, son. Let's let his honor and Mr. Anderson deal with the important stuff."

Tom quickly rose and followed the sheriff outside chambers before the judge could say anything else. They were in a short hallway that connected to a door that opened to the bottom floor of the rotunda, likely full of people curious about what the hell was happening. Tom wasn't sure he wanted to go that way but the only other place to go was back into chambers and he sure as hell wasn't going back in there.

The sheriff put his hand on Tom's arm and looked up at him. "Now, take a deep breath, Mr. Jarrell."

Tom did that very thing and then sighed.

"You know that was all for show, doncha?"

Tom shook his head.

The sheriff grinned. "When the order for the new

Grand Jury came down yesterday, his honor was screaming at Anderson all afternoon, or that was what I heard. If I were you, I'd pay attention to that last little thing Judge Frederick said."

Tom frowned. "What was that?"

"How he was trying to get the attention of the only person who was capable of doing anything."

Tom was completely confused. "I don't understand."

"Son, he was talking about you. Look, we have something like a perfect storm here. Between the problem with the Quince grand jury and the new driver's license rules going into effect today—"

"What new rules?"

The sheriff laughed. "You really must be in your own little world. The state's requiring all drivers to take a new driving test or pay a buck if they don't renew their licenses by 5 p.m. today and you know how cheap most folks around here are. There's huge lines all over the state as a result and, son, I'm stretched to the limit. So is Daytona P.D. So, it's up to you and Ronnie Grisham to find out where Leland Johnson is. That's what the judge was blowing his top about."

"But, why did he threaten me with contempt?"

The sheriff grinned and then said, "You ever seen him with his kids?"

"No."

"Well, he's all smiles until one of them crosses the line. Then he brings the house down on 'em. Look," he said with a sigh. "All that he's doing is telling you is to get your ass in gear. He's not gonna cite you with contempt." Shrugging, the sheriff said, "Even if he did, you'd be out in 24 hours once the paper got the whole story." The sheriff winked and said, "And, believe me, son, they will."

Tom nodded, confused as ever but with a clear idea about what to do next.

Chapter 15

Mayer & Thornton
415 Main Street
Wednesday, October 1, 1947
Half past 10 in the morning

Ronnie had driven much too fast but they made it back to Daytona Beach in record time. Tom had an unpleasant feeling of déjà vu as he walked into the street-level lobby of his old office.

When she saw him, Minnie Otey looked at him in alarm. "Why aren't you at the courthouse?"

"Leland Johnson skipped."

She stood and walked around the desk. Looking up at him, she quietly said, "And I can't find Mr. Thornton. He's not answering his phone. And the police and the sheriff are saying they can't send anyone to his house."

"They're all busy," said Tom. "Are you OK, Minnie?" She was just about the only person he respected at Mayer & Thornton. She was in her early 60s, kept her hair colored a light brown, and knew where all the bodies were buried.

Putting her hands on her hips, she shook her head. "I am worried sick. This place is going to hell in a handbasket." She put her left hand on her chest. "And I just got a call from the hospital that Eugene Mayer slipped into a coma and they don't know if he'll ever wake up."

Tom sighed. He felt like too many things were happening at once.

"I have a terrible feeling about Otis." That was Mr. Thornton's middle name. Minnie was the only one allowed to use it, as far as Tom knew.

Tom put his hand on her shoulder and said, "We'll find Mr. Thornton."

"And what about Leland Johnson?"

"He's the least of my worries."

She nodded. "It would serve Mervyn Anderson right if he did skip and isn't dead, which is what he deserves, considering what he did to his own son."

Tom was confused. "What's that about Mr. Anderson?"

"Didn't you know he didn't object at arraignment when Eugene asked for Leland Johnson to be released on his own recognizance?"

Tom shook his head. "No, ma'am."

She gave him a small smile. Putting her hand on his arm, she said, "You were the best lawyer we ever had around here. Eugene told me he was going to re-hire you after you got Howie Kirkpatrick off. I knew you were too smart to come back..." She looked around the building. "Of course, you could probably buy this practice for a song." She wore her glasses on a gold chain around her neck that dangled across her mostly flat chest. Fingering them, she added, "And I heard you got married on Monday night."

Tom nodded, not knowing what else to do.

"Well, I completely understand."

Tom felt his eyes widen in surprise. "You do?"

"Of course." She looked around, although there was no one out front. "You're still a young man and she's a pretty young thing. It isn't right for you to be a widower for the rest of your life."

Tom wordlessly nodded.

...

L.O. Thornton's wife had died back before Ronnie had moved Sarah and Missy to Daytona Beach. Ronnie wasn't sure, but he thought he'd heard Mrs. Thornton had passed away in 1939.

The old man lived in a house at the corner where Peninsula ended at University, across from the abandoned Seabreeze Golf Course. To Ronnie's mind, the house was a holdover from the good ole days before the land bust of the late 20s. It had a round center with two short wings, one pointing north and the other west.

He bounded up the front steps with Tom slowly bringing up the rear. His pal was obviously having a hard time dealing with all the latest, not that Ronnie blamed him. There was a lot of shit going on and it was hard to take all of it in.

But Ronnie's way was to jump into action. Damn the torpedoes. That sort of thing. He vigorously banged on the front door and then stepped back in surprise as the door opened right up.

Tom pulled on his elbow. "Wait."

Ronnie nodded and stepped back to let his pal get around him.

Using his handkerchief, Tom pushed the door all the way open. "Mr. Thornton?"

Receiving no answer, Ronnie followed Tom into the circular living room. Looking around at the sparse room, barely furnished with only a few pieces that easily came right out of the 1890s, including a faded red love seat, Ronnie spied something that immediately caught his attention. He knelt on the threadbare Persian rug at the base of the circular stair. He'd seen something red. At first, he thought it might be part of the pattern, but it soon became obvious that it wasn't. Looking closer, he said, "Blood."

Next to him, Tom pointed to the second step, painted a light yellow that was slowly peeling, and said, "There's more there."

Standing, Ronnie leaned forward and touched one of the three crimson drops. "Dry."

Tom sighed. He looked around the room and then at Ronnie. "I guess we know where Mr. Thornton is."

Ronnie nodded. "It's OK, bud. Just follow me." He slowly and carefully walked up the steps with Tom right behind him.

The stairs opened directly into a circular bedroom which had windows facing in all directions except west. The room was bright and airy and would have been magnificent except for the fact that, on the bed, whose headboard leaned against the west wall, lay the blood-soaked body of Mr. L.O. Thornton.

Ronnie looked closely at the body while Tom walked over to the windows that faced the beach four blocks east. After getting a good look, Ronnie said, "Stabbed. And he didn't resist, as far as I can tell, although I don't really know."

"Leland Johnson again?"

"That would be my guess but why?"

Tom sighed. "Maybe Mr. Thornton wanted in on some of the action that Mr. Mayer was getting a cut of."

Ronnie walked over and leaned against his pal. "This isn't your fault."

"He didn't know Leland Johnson was cashing out until I told him yesterday morning."

Ronnie wrapped his arms around his pal. "But you didn't bring Leland over here with a knife..."

Tom pulled away. "I have to call the police."

Ronnie nodded to himself as Tom slowly walked down the stairs.

. . .

Back at Mayer & Thornton on Main Street, Tom walked up to Minnie. She took one look at his face and covered her mouth with her left hand. "Is he...?"

Tom nodded. "I'm afraid so, Minnie."

She shook her head. "Did Leland Johnson kill him?"

"Probably. I left Ronnie Grisham at the house. The police don't know when they'll be able to send someone out, so I left him there to make sure no one disturbs the scene."

Minnie looked up at him, her eyes red. "Good Lord. Eugene just passed. I just got off the phone with Norma."

"How was she?" asked Tom, following a kind of internal script his mother had taught him and that Sarah had reinforced.

"She sounded relieved more than anything else."

Tom nodded, again just following the rules. Be nice. Smile. Ask simple questions. Try to comfort the bereaved. Don't push. Just be kind.

Minnie looked around the room. "I wonder what will happen around here."

Tom wished Ronnie was with him. He wanted that embrace that Ronnie had offered him in Mr. Thornton's house that Tom had foolishly walked away from.

He was never going to make that mistake again. In the middle of all the madness, that thought was like a bright light that he could rely on.

"Would you be interested in moving here and taking over?" asked Minnie, almost to herself.

Tom simply replied, "I don't know."

. . .

Tom parked his car in front of the Kress five and dime about half a block south of the office. He slowly got out, remembering his briefcase at the last moment, and then closed the car door. Walking a few steps, he passed the photographer's studio and then stopped in front of Duval Jewelers. Looking in the window, he wondered if that would be a good place to buy wedding rings for Pauline and Bessie.

The night before, while sharing that kind of quiet chat between lovemaking moments that Tom loved so much, Ronnie had suggested they buy matching rings for Pauline and Bessie so the two girls could look at them and think of them as what they really were—rings that bound them together as wife and wife. When Ronnie had said that, Tom had laughed. He was still tickled by how Judge Perkins had called Ronnie his husband.

Looking at the different pieces in the window, Tom wondered if Sarah had ever stood there, in that same spot, and wanted anything for herself that Tom would never have been able to afford. He couldn't imagine her doing that but, then again, there was a lot about Sarah he didn't know.

"Looking for anything in particular?"

Tom glanced up. A middle-aged man with a little paunch was standing just outside the door and watching him with a solicitous smile. Shaking his head, Tom said, "I have a couple of ideas, but I'm late getting back to the office. I'll come by later."

The man nodded. "Of course. Stop by anytime. We'll be happy to help you." He frowned slightly. "Mr. Jarrell, is it?"

Tom nodded and moved his briefcase over to his left hand so he could shake with his right.

"I'm the manager, Mr. Dykeman. Ask for me and I'll be happy to help." He paused with another frown. "Aren't you supposed to be in DeLand and in court today?"

Tom nodded. "There was an unexpected development."

The man nodded thoughtfully. "That's the only thing we can ever expect, isn't it?"

"What?" asked Tom, not sure what Mr. Dykeman meant.

"The unexpected. That's the only real constant in life. Some people say change is the only constant. But I say it's the unexpected."

Tom nodded and said, "I think you may be right."

...

As he slowly walked up the stairs, Tom could hear Marveen on the phone.

"I don't know, Mother. I haven't seen either of them today."

Tom stumbled through the open front door, feeling as if he couldn't take one more step.

Marveen looked up, startled. "Mr. Jarrell just walked in. I'll call you back."

Tom collapsed into one of the chairs by the wall and put his head in his hands.

After a moment, he heard Marveen say, "I went ahead and called the Charlotte airport this morning when I didn't see Inez Johnson's name in the paper this smorning. Turns out, she flew back to New York and wasn't on the plane that crashed."

"Oh," said Tom without looking up.

"And you received a letter about twenty minutes ago. It came special delivery."

"OK."

"I opened it but didn't read it, I promise."

"OK."

She sat down next to him and whispered, "It's from Leland Johnson."

> Mr. Jarrell,
>
> By the time you read this, I will be long gone and I doubt you or anyone will be able to find me.
>
> I wasn't going to do this, but I want you to know what happened since you had the misfortune to be appointed my lawyer. I hope Judge Frederick thinks long and hard about what he did to you. I don't like you but I wouldn't wish me on my worst enemy. Ha Ha Ha
>
> You told Thornton that I was cashing out. He got greedy and wanted his cut of what Mayer was handling for me. He went to the bank, my bank, my Daddy's precious, precious bank, and withdrew all the money that Mayer had collected for me. It came to just over a hundred grand. I graciously let Thornton keep half of it.
>
> Then last night I walked right into his house and killed him. It was simple.

Found a knife in the kitchen and walked up the stairs. He was drunk, I suppose. He never even woke up as I stabbed him again and again. When you do it once, it's easy to do it again. He left his brief-case downstairs, right on top of that old red settee. Can you imagine? Fifty grand in cash just out there in a house with an unlocked door.

That's really all there is to it. I'm leaving lousy Daytona Beach and all the lousy tourists and the idiots at the Chamber of Commerce and the secret gambling halls and the ridiculous people like you who think I'm the worst thing to happen since... Well, I guess I am the worst thing to happen there. Makes me kind of famous, I suppose. I hope you enjoy the rest of your scummy, nasty life at the World's Most Famous Beach.

Leland Johnson

Author's Note

Thank you for reading this Daytona Beach story!

I had a lot of fun writing this book and I hope you enjoyed reading it!

As with all my novels, this story and its characters came out of thin air. I'm very grateful for that.

. . .

Books about Tom & Ronnie are usually available around the 10th of each month. If you would like to be notified when the next volume is available, you can subscribe here:

http://frankwbutterfield.com/subscribe

Acknowledgments

Many, many thanks to a fabulous group of beta readers: Justene Adamec, L.R. Bombard, Art Foley, David M., and Teresa Price along with several other wonderful folks. These books really would not be possible without you.

Very special thanks to Edward Lane for his patronage of this book!

Kim Dolce at the City Island branch of the Volusia County Public Library once again offered several wonderful suggestions.

Many thanks, again, to Fayn LeVeille, Director of the Halifax Historical Museum on Beach Street in Daytona Beach. She graciously and generously helped me with a number of questions.

Additional thanks to Priscilla Cardwell for her insights into Judge Herbert Frederick.

For insight into the history of Stetson University and its College of Law, I referred to *Florida's First Law School: A History of Stetson University College of Law* by Michael I. Swygert and W. Gary Vause.

Justene Adamec offered some excellent insight into the legal aspects of this book, particularly the many conflicts of interest Tom encounters.

Any mistakes in regard to the law and the history of the law school at Stetson are entirely my own.

Historical Notes

I want to keep this part very brief for this book. The vast majority of the characters in this book are fictional. However, there are actual historical persons whom I've mentioned in these first two books:

Mary McLeod Bethune - Founder of Bethune-Cookman University

Judge Herbert Frederick - Volusia County Circuit Court Judge

Sherriff Alex D. Littlefield - Volusia County Sherriff's Office

Police Chief Thomas Johnson - Daytona Beach Police Department

Ray Jordan - lawyer who practiced in DeLand

Ray Jordan - his daughter (yes, with the same name) and librarian for Stetson University College of Law

Credits

Yesteryear Font (headings) used with permission under SIL Open Font License, Version 1.1. Copyright © 2011 by Brian J. Bonislawsky DBA Astigmatic (AOETI). All rights reserved.

Gentium Book Basic Font (body text) used with permission under the SIL Open Font License, Version 1.1. Copyright © 2002 by J. Victor Gaultney. All rights reserved.

Gladifilthefte Font (cover) by Tup Wanders used under a Creative Commons license by attribution.

Langdon Font (cover) provided freely by XLN Telecom.

My Underwood Font (telegrams) used with permission. Copyright © 2009 by Tension Type. All rights reserved.

More Information

Be the first to know about new releases:

frankwbutterfield.com

Made in the USA
Middletown, DE
07 December 2018